# *Hard To Love*

## Book #4 in the Rockin' Country Series

## By Laramie Briscoe

Edited by: Lindsay Gray Hopper
Cover Art by: Kari Ayasha, Cover to Cover Designs
Proofread by: Dawn Bourgeois
Formatting: Paul Salvette, BB ebooks
Photography by: KKeeton Designs
Cover Models: Sager & Faith

Heaven Hill Series
Meant To Be
Out of Darkness
Losing Control
Worth The Battle
Dirty Little Secret
Second Chance Love
Rough Patch
Beginning of Forever

Rockin' Country Series
Only The Beginning
One Day at a Time
The Price of Love
Full Circle

The Red Bird Trail Trilogy
Flagger
In-Tune
Collision

Guitarist
Recovering Addict
Man Of Few Emotions

Jared Winston has spent much of his adult life in the public eye as the lead guitarist for the hugely popular rock band Black Friday. Presented with temptations from every side and dealing with the mess that was his childhood, he's been known to indulge in excess.

One such excess almost killed him when he overdosed on Halloween.

The experience left him wanting to turn his life around, and it left everyone else in his life struggling, trying to balance the dual emotions of fear and anger.

One person, in particular, isn't sure at all what she wants to do.

Friend
Glutton For Punishment
Giver Of Love Not Returned

Michelle Sanders has made her living as the assistant to the country music star Harmony Stewart. As a personal assistant, she thrives under structure and is always the one to fight for what her friend deserves.

When she met Jared, she took a chance on imperfection – she knew his history – and was warned. That is a chance she's not sure will ever pay off.

Her perfect structure was blown to hell on the night Jared OD'd, and now she has to decide if she wants to risk her heart again.

Love is a game. It's a chance taken; a roll of the dice. Shell gambles, but never in her wildest imagination did she think that the person who loves her would make it so hard for her to love him back.

# Dedication

To anyone who's ever been put in a place where it's hard
to love a special person in your life…..

# Prologue

J ARED WINSTON TOOK in the scene before him, wondering what had become of his life. Was this it? Was this what he'd worked so hard for? In front of him lay a mirror, on it were three lines of cocaine, to the left was a hundred dollar bill that he was going to use to snort the powder up his nose. After he did those three lines, he was going to change. He was going to go to rehab—an overdose would do that to you—it would make you believe it was time for things to change. But first, he had to give into the vice one last time. He had to feel that high, he had to taste the drug deep in his throat. He knew without a doubt if he did any of it again—he would die.

He shut off his phone; it had been ringing consistently every half-hour. The woman he loved was trying to save him. She thought it was her job, her duty, to make things better for him. Little did she know he had to do that for himself. If he didn't make this decision and stick to it, he would be dead in weeks; he knew that—they all knew that.

With a pounding heart, he leaned forward and put the rolled up bill between his thumb and forefinger. In slow motion, he put one end of the bill to the glass of the mirror and the other end to his nose. Once it was there, he inhaled and pulled back, wiping his nose as he sniffled.

One line down, two to go. The feeling of euphoria wasn't immediate; he was much too numb to the effects for that. His tolerance was sky high, and that was the scary part.

The second line went much like the first. This time, he felt a little shaky, and he hated himself for needing so much.

On the third hit, he felt it. It hit him like a brick wall. Finally, that feeling only the drug could give him enveloped his body. He didn't allow himself to admit it was the same feeling his girlfriend, Shell, gave him. He didn't allow himself to admit he felt this feeling on stage when he played for an arena full of people.

No. He told himself, as he had for years, that the only way he could feel was when he took a hit.

It was time to come to some realizations. It was time to fix himself. It was past time to be the man everyone told him he could be.

It was time to grow up, face his demons, and stop making excuses for why he kept fucking up. Responsibility was his. It was time to own it.

*Three Months Later*

JARED GLANCED AT the message that had been relayed to him inside the rehab center. He'd been on good behavior and he'd been allowed to use his cell phone. The text that had come through made him smile and made his heart happy. He was an uncle. His best friend was now a father, and he hadn't been there to see it. He understood that he had to get better; he wouldn't be allowed to be around the baby if he wasn't. That had been one of the motivators for him getting help this time.

"Jared, it's time for group."

Group. His least favorite part of the day. He was expected to share parts of himself that he had never told other people about. Add to that it was a requirement, not a request, and the basic part of him that resisted everything fought back. But he had to admit it was helping. He wasn't feeling like he was about to crawl out of his skin anymore, he wasn't searching for a way out. Even though this was a resigned kind of acceptance, he would take it.

Pulling his hoodie over his head, he made his way through the building and out to the courtyard before entering the adjacent building and walking into the first classroom. He took the first seat, like he was known to do, and waited for the rest of the members to come in.

The leader had a seat and waited for everyone to get situated. Jared watched as the room filled up, and then he waited for them to call his name.

"Jared, we ended with you last session. Let's pick

back up." The leader glanced over at him. "What would you say your downfall was?"

This shit was so fucking uncomfortable. "I've had more than one," he admitted. "The first one was thinking I could make my parents into what I wanted them to be. They didn't want kids, they got me, they didn't know how to deal with a kid who had ADD, and I can admit now that I was a holy terror. Then everybody felt sorry for me, no one wanted to tell me no, because they saw how my parents treated me. Fast forward a few years, and I was in a world-famous band and nobody dared tell me no."

"What forced you to see that?"

"Hurting everybody I love, including my best friend, the woman I love, and the band that took me in like family. I have to get better." He rubbed the hoodie over his head. "I know myself. I'm going to die if I don't, and I have way too much to live for."

The leader clapped his hands together. "*That* is exactly what we love to hear, Jared. Now are you ready to fight?"

Was he? He'd asked himself the question a couple of times, and each time he came up with the same answer. "Fuck yeah, I'm ready to fight."

"Then let's fight together."

# Chapter One

W EARING A SUIT felt odd. Jared tried to remember the last time he'd actually worn one. Maybe something that the band had to do together? But tonight, he knew he had to do it. Putting his best foot forward was important for him at this point in his recovery, and he wanted Shell to realize he was serious.

Garrett had done him a solid and told him Shell would be watching baby EJ while he and Hannah were out on their Valentine's Day date. He gripped the flowers he held in his hand, wondering what in the hell she would do. There was a small part of him that hoped she would welcome him with open arms; there was another, larger, part of him that wanted her to fight. He wanted her to make him work for it. He deserved to work for it. The shit he'd put her through? He'd be lucky if she didn't slam the door in his face.

As he approached the door, his palms were sweaty in a way they hadn't been before. He'd played in front of hundreds of thousands of people and not batted an eyelash, but this woman could bring him to his knees.

He turned back from the door and walked around in a circle twice. His heart pounded in his throat, and it was in this moment that he badly wanted to take a hit of something. It didn't matter what it was, but he needed something to calm him down.

Instead, he took a deep breath and ran through all the tips he'd gotten in his time at rehab. He went through all his rituals, looking ahead at the bigger picture, pushing back the way his mouth watered for the hit of something. He pictured the look on Shell's face when she'd finally be able to accept him into her life again. Being a part of EJ's life, being a part of Black Friday. Those were the end game, and that's what he knew he had to remember.

Taking another deep breath, he approached the door and finally let his knuckles connect to the wood. He waited for what felt like a hundred years, and when the door opened, he fought to make the words come forward.

She looked even better than he remembered. Her hair was longer and blonder than it had been when he'd last seen her. She was smaller, and he knew part of that was the stress he'd caused her. For a minute there was a smile on her face, and she gave him an adoring look.

"What are you doing here?"

Jared thrust a bouquet of roses towards her and spoke from his heart. "I'm here to do whatever it takes to win you back and prove to you just how much I love you."

When the door slammed in his face, he wasn't surprised. In fact, it made him chuckle, and a smile tugged at the corners of his mouth. His girl had balls. His girl was going to make him work for it, and if that's what he needed to do, that's what he was going to do.

He put the roses on the concrete, leaning them up against the door. Hopefully, she would read the note he left inside. Hopefully, she would give him a second chance.

SHELL FUMED AS she walked from the foyer, back into the living room. She wanted to scream or punch something, but she didn't want to wake up the baby, who was sleeping peacefully. Grabbing the baby monitor and her purse, she went to the back porch, leaving the door ajar as a secondary precaution.

Her hands shook as she rifled through her purse, pulling out her half-smoked pack of cigarettes. This was a habit not many people knew about. She only did it when she absolutely needed the stress relief. It took her a few tries, but she managed to light the tip, inhaling deeply as she let the nicotine spread through her body.

How could he come here and expect that things would be just as they left them? She hadn't seen him in months. She laughed, and even she realized how crazed it sounded. This was it; she'd finally driven herself insane trying to keep up with him. The sad thing was? She wanted him. There was nothing more that she wanted than to throw herself in his arms, let him wrap her up and make it all better.

She lifted the filter of the cigarette up to her mouth and held it between her lips as she grabbed her phone. This was torture, but she continued to do it to herself when she missed him more than she imagined she could. As she blew out smoke, she scrolled through the pictures on her phone.

There, she went through the years of their time together, starting from when they'd first starting hanging out in secret, to them officially dating, to a few days before the incident that sent him to rehab. Not all of those pictures represented happy times. They'd had their fair share of hard times, but she'd always known they would be together at the end of the day.

Until they weren't.

As much as she missed the Jared who stared back at her from the early days, she wasn't sure she could put her heart out there again. It had broken her when she'd watched him fighting to live. Even now, sometimes when she closed her eyes, she could hear Garrett screaming at him to breathe. She knew without a doubt she couldn't handle another scene like that.

And now he was back. He looked great, healthy, and happy. He would stay that way long enough to fool her, long enough to lull her into a false sense of security, and then he would go off the rails again.

Unless he didn't.

And that's where she worried that she would let the possible happiness slip her by, and she'd never be able to reclaim it.

Nothing about Jared's love was easy—including giving hers to him.

She took a last hit off her cigarette and stood up as EJ began to cry. Walking back into the house, her shoulders were heavier than they'd been in a long time.

# Chapter Two

JARED SIGHED AS he heard the alarm blaring in his ear. Reaching over, he grabbed his phone, sliding the snooze button, giving himself five more minutes. This was a ritual. He would do this two more times, and by then, he would be awake enough so that he could pull himself out of bed and think about beginning his day. He'd never been a morning person, but one of the things he'd learned in rehab was that he did better if he faced the morning head-on.

*"Get up, rock star."*

*He hated the way she said rock star, almost like it was a bad word. He hadn't asked for what happened with him and Black Friday—they were fucking lucky. Only a handful of the bands that formed every year had been able to reach the point of success they were at.*

*"Leave me the fuck alone." He tried to pull the covers back up over his eyes.*

*"Not going to happen today. It's time for you to get up, get out, and face the sun. You're living in the dark, man," the rehab*

*nurse said, pulling back the covers again.*

*Was she right? Was that what he was really doing? He tried to think of his life, tried to think of his schedule. Most of it occurred at night—hell, almost everything they did as a band happened late afternoon into the overnight hours. It made it easy for him to sleep his life away. The only time he made an exception was when he knew Shell would be there.*

*Immediately his thoughts went to Garrett. When he and Hannah had gotten serious, he'd watched his best friend make sure he was up and at 'em—always with her, always with a cup of coffee in his hand. It hadn't mattered how tired he was, he made time for her. He was selfless.*

*Unlike the selfish bastard lying in the bed.*

*"C'mon, Jared. It's time to face life head-on. Once it becomes a habit, you'll appreciate it."*

He wasn't sure that he appreciated it, per se, but it did start him off on a better foot than sleeping until noon. Now he had a schedule. He had to have a schedule. If he didn't, he seemed to worry about what to do with his time—and he tried not to veer from that schedule.

His text went off, interrupting his snooze he'd set. "Fuck it," he groaned, sitting up. Grabbing his phone, he saw a text from Garrett.

*Gonna be a few minutes late. Want me to bring you one of those protein bars I got from the farmers' market?*

Jared's mouth watered. That thing tasted like a fucking candy bar. The Nashville Farmers' Market beat California's bar none.

*It's the least you can do, asshole. I was enjoying my fifteen minutes of snooze.*

His and Garrett's friendship was getting back to normal, although it was a new normal. They weren't close in the same way they had been before, but Jared was okay with that. He knew he had to prove to everyone that he was serious. Thankfully, Garrett was willing to be an active participant in his recovery, and they worked out together daily. Sometimes Hannah came, and honestly, those were his favorite days, because she tended to talk about Shell. Through Hannah, he vicariously lived Shell's life.

*Quit your bitchin'. I'll be there in about an hour. EJ woke us up puking, so it's been kind of a hectic morning.*

Immediately Jared gave him an out.

*If you need to stay home and be dad, that's cool. I can do this on my own.*

And he could, but it would be hard. Any deviation from his schedule, even now, bothered him.

*Never. I'll be there. Han knows how important this is.*

Hannah had not only saved Garrett, but it looked like she was helping save him too. Feeling more emotional than he had a right too, he got out of bed and walked towards the shower. It would do wonders in waking him up, and give him a few minutes to reflect on how his life had changed.

"You got it. Five more!"

Jared grunted as he pushed the barbell over his head, listening to Garrett count him down. After this, they would do two miles on the treadmill, and then their workout would be done.

"You're done," Garrett told him, putting his hand out to help him off the bench.

Gratefully, Jared took his friends hand and let him pull him up. He realized that was kind of a metaphor for his life the past few months. Friends had been lifting and pulling him up.

"You're quiet today," Garrett mentioned as they made their way over to the treadmills.

He nodded, setting his for the pace he liked to keep. Both of them started the run and had been at it for a few minutes when Jared found the right words to answer.

"Yeah, I saw Shell last night." His voice was quiet.

"I figured. I told you she'd be alone, and then Hannah and I saw the flowers when we came home."

"So she never picked them up?" Jared asked carefully. He didn't want to sound gutted over that, but in actuality he was. He'd thought maybe she would go back out and get them after he left.

He shook his head. "No, but Han grabbed them. She

kept the card and letter, and then she put the flowers in a vase. They aren't going to waste, my friend."

"Can you make sure she gives the card and letter to Shell when she's ready for it?"

"I can." Garrett took a drink from his water bottle. "I'm sorry it didn't work out for you last night; I hoped that it would."

"Yeah." Jared sighed. "Me too." he pulled the hem of his shirt up to his forehead and wiped away the sweat gathered there. "But I can't use a magic eraser to wipe out all the shit I've done to her over the years. This is gonna take some work on my part."

Garrett wanted to tell him that Shell wasn't perfect either. She was going to have to work too. Relationships weren't one-sided; they required that both people be present and willing to put the work in. He knew, though, that Jared was going to have to figure that out for himself.

"You're doing great," Garrett encouraged. "Things will fall in the way they're supposed to. You look better than you ever have, you're happier than I've seen you in a long time, and everything else will work itself out."

Jared knew Garrett was right, but that didn't mean he didn't want it to work out right now.

JARED GLANCED AT his watch and cursed. He was running a few minutes late—and that bothered him now—something that hadn't before. He'd gotten engrossed in his writing, and had to rush through a shower, and then race across town.

"Don't shut the door," he yelled as he ran towards the auditorium.

"You were almost late, Winston."

"Almost only counts in horseshoes and hand grenades." He grinned, squeezing himself through the opening.

Entering the room, he saw faces that he saw at least two or three times a week. He tried to make as many meetings as he could—whether they were NA or AA. They both benefited him. Walking to the back, he had a seat and stretched his long legs out. He'd abused them at the gym today, and they were a little sore. Up in front, someone stepped up, welcoming them.

Finally, his favorite part came. These little snippets of words were his comfort, his belief, and the motto with which he lived his life now. He had to. Jared Winston finally wanted to live.

*God, grant me the serenity to accept the things I cannot change, the courage to change the things I can, and the wisdom to know the difference.*

# Chapter Three

"**W**HAT? I GOT a B?" Shell questioned, wrinkling her nose.

Hannah laughed as she turned towards her friend, a bowl of cereal in her hand. "You're the only person I know who gripes because they got a B on a paper. Anyone else would be excited. They would be jumping from the rooftops with joy. But not my Shell; no, she's ticked off."

"I worked hard on that paper," Shell protested. "I went above and beyond—they told us to cite three sources. I cited six for fuck's sake."

"Maybe you went a little overboard?"

This wasn't the first time someone had mentioned that word to her, and she did have a tendency to have to be the best at everything she did. It was a strength and a weakness. "That's possibly true, but I don't think I should be *punished* for it."

"Only you would think a B is a punishment."

It was hard to explain to people who hadn't lived her life in the past few months. School, doing Harmony's social media, and demo singing were all she had. They were the only things that had not only kept her head on straight but kept her from going crazy. When Jared had gone to rehab and then refused to speak to her, she'd lost not only one of her best friends, but her partner in life. It had been a devastating blow, and one she hadn't been prepared for.

She shrugged. "I am who I am."

They heard the garage door open, and a minute later, Garrett came through the garage into the kitchen. "Ladies, how's it going?"

"Shell's being punished. She got a B on a paper. And I'm finally sitting down to eat some breakfast. EJ is, for the moment, asleep."

"For shame." He gave Shell a glance, throwing her a face. "A B is the end of the world for you, isn't it? This one," he put his arms around Hannah and pulled her close, "is my little goodie-two-shoes. You," he pointed to her, "are my braniac."

"I didn't come here to be made fun of." She threw a waded up piece of paper in his direction.

"Love you too, Shell." He stared at her for a few minutes, waiting for her to ask the question he knew she wanted to. When she didn't, he answered it anyway. "Jared's good, by the way."

"I didn't ask."

"Doesn't mean that you don't want to know."

Damn him. She seethed inside. Garrett always did this to her. He offered information she didn't ask for a reason. His grand scheme was to the get the two of them back together, but she wasn't done with her anger yet. She still had a lot to work through, and every time he offered her a glimpse into Jared's life, it broke another barrier.

"Whatever, anyway, I gotta go. If I don't leave now, I'm gonna be late."

"Where are you going?" Hannah asked, tilting her head to the side, her eyes raking over her best friend.

"I'm recording some demos over on Music Row. Not a big deal, just something to get me out of the house."

She didn't wait for them to ask her any more questions or offer her any advice. Instead she grabbed up her notebook, laptop, and purse quickly. "I hope EJ feels better, and if you two need anything, let me know."

Turning on her heel, she made her way to the front door.

"Love you, Shell," she heard Hannah yell.

"Love you too," she answered back as she closed the door.

Once she did, she leaned against it, trying to catch her breath. For some reason, her heart pounded, and she felt like she would pass out. Was this how news of Jared was going to affect her from now on? Was she going to have a case of the vapors? Dear God, she hoped not.

One man shouldn't have the right to affect her this much, especially when she'd been doing her best to put him out of her head before last night. Seeing him last night, it had conjured up all of the good memories, because he'd looked so good. All the times he'd been sweet and loving. It was easy to forget the times he'd been an asshole when all she could see was the clearness of his eyes, the easiness of his smile.

But she knew with him, he could change in an instant. Something could happen and it would send him back over the edge if he hadn't learned the proper way to deal with it in rehab. She wondered if he had, but that was another part of his life he'd kept separate from her, she reminded herself.

It sucked, but sometimes Jared only wanted to be in a relationship when it was good for him. When it benefited what he wanted to do. She was working hard not to make herself easily available for him—which was why she'd slammed the door in his face last night. But damn if that hadn't hurt her in ways she hadn't intended.

When she'd gotten home last night, she'd thought about the whole situation, over and over. What if this had been his cry for help to her, and what if she'd just shut him down? What if he really had changed and she wasn't willing to give him another chance?

There were no right or wrong answers, but she knew with everything in her that she had to go with her gut. Her gut was telling her to make him work for it. Make him show her how much she meant to him. And maybe by him doing that, she could show him how much he meant to her.

# Chapter Four

J ARED MOVED HIS head around on his shoulders, trying to work the muscles of his neck. They were tight, his whole body was tight. This was the first time he'd been with the guys as a group since he'd come back from rehab. Individually, he'd spoken to each of his band members and quietly asked for forgiveness.

Standing on the Nashville practice stage, he felt butterflies. He had never felt butterflies in his life, but standing here, he did. Taking a deep breath, he tried to calm his rapidly beating heart and focus on the job at hand. All they were doing here was running through their show twice before they would embark on a small Asian tour. Small by their caliber. Twelve dates in eighteen days. It would be grueling, but that's how Black Friday did things.

"You doing okay?" Garrett asked as he walked over to his friend.

It amazed Jared how quickly they all became their personas. Gone was the happy-go-lucky dad and father. In its place was their badass-looking Reaper. He'd let his beard grow in the past few days, and coupled with his bandana, backwards hat, and aviators, he looked like someone you didn't want to meet in a dark alley. Jared also knew that he looked the part of Train. His once long hair was now freshly shaven on the sides, giving him a Mohawk, and he wore a tank top that showcased the muscles he'd won in rehab, tattoos out. He looked at Brad and Chris, realizing they were ready for battle too.

"I'm good." He nodded. Although he wasn't sure. He was scared to death.

"Alright, let's get this started."

Chris counted off the beat with his drumsticks, and immediately, he went into their first song. He played from muscle memory, closing his eyes, letting the music wash over him. This was the one thing he hadn't been allowed to do in rehab. They hadn't let him have his guitar. At first it had felt like a punishment, and he'd resented every moment of it, but then he'd understood. He'd needed to become Jared there, and deal with himself—not Train, who everybody worshiped and adored. He had to become comfortable in his own skin, without his guitar being his shield. In order to embrace the program, he'd had to let his guard go and laying his guitar down was the first step in doing that. But damn, this felt good.

He didn't even realize how long he'd been playing, couldn't tell anyone how many songs they'd gone through when he opened his eyes, but he knew it'd been a while. Garrett had gotten rid of his shirt, as had Chris. Jared looked down at himself and saw sweat pouring from his arms onto his hands; his tank top was soaked, and when he looked out, where their techs sat, he now noticed Hannah and Shell. He wished he knew how long they'd been there, but it was a relief to see her. It had been two weeks since Valentine's Day, and she'd managed to avoid him every time he'd tried to run into her. She wasn't going to get out of here without talking to him today.

"I CAN'T BELIEVE you brought me here," Shell hissed to Hannah as they entered the sound stage area.

"I did not trick you," Hannah protested as she made sure that EJ wore his special ear coverings before pushing his stroller through. "I told you I was going to see Garrett. He's in a band with Jared. Did you not think that meant Jared too?"

Shell wasn't sure what she'd thought it meant, but it wasn't this. The two of them were quiet as they went to one of the couches set up for people to observe them. They waved at Rick, Black Friday's manager, and had a seat at the one furthest in the back.

"Just enjoy this," Hannah said as she rocked the stroller back and forth with her foot. "It's been a while since both of us have seen them perform."

Shell sighed. It had been a long time, and performing Jared was one of her favorite Jared's. The way the man played the guitar was breathtaking. He lost himself in the chords like many singers lost themselves in the words. Immediately her eyes went to his fingers as they worked the fretboard; they played that thing like they played her body. His eyes were closed, giving her the freedom to look at him, really look at him. He looked good, better than she remembered him ever looking. Gone was the gauntness she'd seen the night he'd OD'd. He'd filled out, and it looked damn good on him. He'd never be Garrett big, but he was healthy and strong. That in itself was sexy. Allowing her eyes to travel up his torso to his neck, she breathed slightly heavier when she saw the tendons of his neck pulled tight, supporting his thrown back head. That was the way he looked when he came inside her, and it heated her up. God, she missed him.

"You okay?"

"Yeah, I'm good," Shell answered, trying to calm her out-of-control pulse.

Hannah grinned at her. "You're giving him this look that says, if you could, you'd go onstage, rip your clothes off, lie down, spread your legs, and say *take me now!*"

"Garrett has been a really bad influence on you. You have no idea what I was thinking. Now go away." She smacked at her friend's hand.

"Oh, I know exactly what you were thinking, and I think I'm blushing from it."

Shell giggled, looking away from Hannah only to have her eyes meet those of Jared. He stared directly at her, almost like he could see straight through her. It was unnerving, especially when Garrett set his mic down and told all of them to take a break.

*Please don't come over here. Please come over here.* Even her subconscious couldn't make a clear-cut decision. She wanted him and she didn't want him. Nothing was ever easy.

That decision was taken away from her when he walked her way, his eyes daring her to turn and walk away. Immediately, it got her back up, and she felt the need to stay. Game on, buddy.

# Chapter Five

"HEY," HE GREETED her quietly, his hands shoved in his pockets.

He looked like a little kid who wasn't sure if he would be welcomed, and that honestly kind of broke her heart. No matter how she felt about him, she wouldn't treat him the way his parents had.

"Hey," she answered back. The words felt foreign to her. They were the first words she'd spoken to him, voluntarily, in months.

"I'm sorry I ambushed you at their house the other night; I knew you wouldn't see me if I asked you too." He pulled his hands out of his pockets and ran them along the shaved sides of his head.

Him, apologizing? Hell had frozen over for sure.

"You're right," she answered. "I wouldn't have seen you; I would have run as far as I could in the other direction, to be honest."

"I deserve that." He rocked back on his heels, trying to find his balance, both spiritually and figuratively.

She tried not to let anger get the better of her. Shell

really didn't want to be one of those women who yelled and blamed, but there were a lot of things she'd held in because he wouldn't allow her to talk to him. There were a lot of things she'd wanted to tell him, and she hadn't been allowed to. Those things had simmered, and now she was worried they were about to boil over.

"You deserve that and a whole lot more, Jared. I'm trying very hard not to blame you, because I know you were in a bad place, probably the worst place you've ever been in your life." She took a deep breath. "And I'm not the kind of person to kick someone when they're down, but you have to understand—you did things to me that I haven't recovered from, and I'm not sure if I will."

"That's fair." He wanted her to feel the way she felt, he wanted her to own her feelings. "But you have to understand that I was going through some things. Still am."

It was then that she shut down, and he saw it. He could tell she was done listening.

"I didn't sign up for the going-through-things Jared." She held her hand up. "I signed up for the going-through-things-as-a-couple Jared."

"I'm trying to apologize to you so that we can move forward," he argued.

She leveled him with a glare. "Move forward? You want to fucking move forward?"

Shell knew she was yelling, and she was aware of most everybody in the room staring at them, but she couldn't stop her voice as it continued to rise.

"You didn't speak to me for months, Jared. Months.

I reached out to you more times than I care to admit to anyone else because it makes me look like a dumbass. I cried over you. I worried over you. I made myself sick over you. And you stand right here and seriously tell me you want to apologize so that we can move forward?" She laughed, crossing her arms over her chest. "That is the biggest line of horse shit I have ever heard in my life."

"Shell…"

"You're not from the South, maybe you don't know what horse shit is. But it's stinky, and it comes in big piles, a lot like what's coming out of your mouth. It builds up."

He let the corner of his mouth tilt in a grin. "It's also used in gardens to make flowers grow."

Instead of losing steam, she gained some. "Oh, kiss my ass."

"I'm trying," he yelled back at her. "If you'd read what I left in those flowers, you'd know what I'm trying to do here."

She turned around in a circle, her eyes catching Hannah's. Hannah knew what she'd gone through, had been there with her through the whole thing. Even pregnant, Hannah had wiped her tears and tried to cheer her up. Tired from being a new mom, she'd pulled herself out of bed and taken Shell places, most of the time dragging EJ along. She owed this not only to herself, but to Hannah. She couldn't give in easily this time.

"It's easy for you to write something, Jared. You're a songwriter. You write beautiful music, and you're well known for it." She ran her fingers through her hair. "What you're not good at is vocalizing feelings, and I used to be okay with that. I used to believe that no matter what, no matter what you didn't say, you still felt it."

"I do," he tried to interrupt her.

"No, unless you can *tell me*, I'm not listening. I'm done with the nonverbal clues and assumptions. Real men…they wear their heart on their sleeve. They have their wife's and son's names tattooed on their back. They aren't afraid to show the world how much they care."

He was quiet, as was the rest of the room.

"You wanna talk about deserving? I deserve that, because Lord knows I've put up with a ton of your shit over the past few years. Love is a two-way street. Respect is a two-way street. This time, I'm hanging on to my dignity. I'm not going the wrong way down a one-way again."

She grabbed her purse and turned to Hannah. "I'll meet you all at dinner, because I still wanna go, but right now I need a couple of minutes to myself."

Helplessly, he watched as she walked away, not sure how to fix this. Not sure if it even could be fixed.

# Chapter Six

"YOU KNOW YOU don't have to go through with this, right?"

Shell met Hannah's eyes in the rearview mirror, thankful her friend said that. They were in Hannah's Land Rover making their way towards a restaurant they all loved in North Nashville. She sat in the back, making sure EJ was preoccupied. Garrett was behind the wheel, chauffeuring them.

"No, I do," she protested. "Jared and I have to learn how to be friends with one another. He's not going to want to give up his family, and neither am I." She shrugged, reaching down to put EJ's pacifier back in his mouth. This kid was a godsend; when things got to be too much, she could always count on him to help her get a perspective.

"Here's the deal." Garrett set down the energy drink he had just taken a sip from. "He's my best friend, and I'm saying this because I do love him. Jared's never had to work for anything in his life. Music comes easy to him. Before you, women came easy to him. I'm proud of you for standing up for yourself. He's got to put the work in. Just like you, I'll make myself as available as I can, but he's got to want to stay clean."

"I worry he'll choose the drugs over me. What if I make him wait too long, what if I'm never able to overcome everything that he and I have been through?"

"That's his loss, sweetheart, not yours. You're the reward, not the consequence. Make him fight; he'll hang on that much tighter."

She wondered if Garrett spoke the truth. All she knew—for sure—was that she was tired. She was tired of fighting for something that could possibly never truly be hers. Wondering when he would find the courage to tell her how he felt. Hoping that for once he would be the one willing to come to her and tell her how he felt first. She was sick of assuming. This time she needed the words, she needed the actions. She needed it all. "I'm tired, Garrett," she told him, knowing that he would understand.

"We all are, but he's got to put the work in too. He can't expect any of us to change our lives to make it easier for him. Life isn't easy. It's work, and in the end, when we put in the time, we get the rewards. None of this is handed to any of us. I work out, I eat right, I get up at night with my son, there are some days I am so exhausted that even these energy drinks don't help, but I do it because it's worth it."

Quietly, Shell asked, "What if I'm not worth it?" Jared not accepting her calls and doing what he had done had really affected her self-esteem.

Hannah turned around sharply. "Stop that right now. You sound like the me from three years ago. You're worth it, and you'll get your mojo back. This is all awkward right now, but give it time. Things will work out."

Shell nodded, but she wasn't so sure.

ADRENALINE WAS HIS drug of choice now; it helped to push the cravings away when they got to be overwhelming. Some counselors had said it was easy to get addicted to this too, because it gave some users the same type of high as drugs.

To Jared, that wasn't true. This high was one he could grab hold of with two hands and face head on. It didn't leave him in the same clothes from yesterday or struggling to remember what he'd done the night before. This was one he could take and then let go.

He shifted gears, accelerating through the Nashville streets as he made his way to the dinner spot for the night. He'd never been one to ride a bike before rehab, but one of the counselors had suggested it as a way for him to clear his head, get a clean slate when the noise got to be too much.

He'd never felt more free in his life than when he was on the back of his bike.

Pulling into the parking lot, he saw Garrett, Hannah, and Shell getting out of Hannah's Land Rover. He caught Shell checking him out, and it made him feel good. She didn't know the person behind the helmet was him; he'd not been able to tell her about his new obsession. Parking next to them, he shut off the bike and took off his helmet, hooking it on the handlebar.

He turned and caught Shell staring at him.

"It's new," he supplied. "Riding helps me clear my head."

She flipped her blonde hair over her shoulder. "I didn't ask."

"No." he winked. "But you wanted to know."

Pursing her lips, she gave him her back and made her way towards the entrance.

Hannah gave him a small smile, grabbing EJ's carrier. "Keep trying. At some point she'll get sick of being a bad-ass chick."

All the guys in the band glanced at each other in shock, and Garrett smile widely.

"Babe, did you just say bad ass?"

She shook her head. "I did, because sometimes you've just gotta." Stepping up to Jared, she stared him down, not turning her eyes away from him. "I'm counting on you to keep at this until she lets her guard down, and if you don't—you're not the man I thought you were."

"I'll accept that." Jared reached out, putting his hand on her shoulder, squeezing it to let her know he understood. "If I give up, I'm not the man I thought I was either."

All five-foot-two of her glared at him. "Then we understand each other."

"Got it, Han."

"Good." She switched EJ's carrier to the other hand. "Then let's go eat. I'm starving."

So was he, and he was looking forward to having Shell in one place. With everybody around, she couldn't get away so easily.

# Chapter Seven

IMMEDIATELY, SHELL RECOGNIZED her mistake in sitting down at the table first. It had left every single seat next to her free. Jared smiled widely as he took the free one on the right-hand side. She wanted to get up and move, but when Garrett and Hannah adjusted chairs so that they could put EJ's carrier between them, she hated to ask them to change what they were doing.

Grabbing the menu the waitress put in front of her, she busied herself studying her options. She wasn't sure why she did, because she always ordered the same thing here, but it gave her something to do besides obsessing over Jared sitting beside her.

She sucked in a breath when his knee hit hers, their thighs close enough to touch under the table. Cutting her eyes at him, she sent what she hoped was a glare, but feared it was more of an invitation. This was the closest she'd been to him since the night he'd been taken to the hospital. Everything about him was familiar, and she'd missed it all. The spiciness of his cologne, the earthy scent of the leather jacket he wore, the way he tapped a beat on the table with his thumb as he browsed the menu.

It was all enough to bring tears to her eyes and make her want to try. She'd missed him so damn much, and now she was fighting with herself, and fighting against him. "I'll be back." She threw her napkin on the table and quickly made her way to the restroom.

"I'M GONNA GO check on her," Hannah told the group quietly, before getting up herself.

Jared watched her go before turning to the group. "I'm sorry. If it'll be easier, I'll go."

"No," Garrett answered. "It's not going to make it any easier. You have to realize that we've all got to work through this. The group of us, we're damaged, and running away isn't going to solve anything. Hannah will bring her back."

"I want her to be here because she wants to be," Jared argued.

Brad laughed. "We all know Shell. If she didn't want to be here, she wouldn't be. Time is going to be your best friend."

"That and your knees," Chris joked. "You're going to need to be on them a lot, like daily, begging for forgiveness."

"I plan on it. I know this isn't going to be easy."

Garrett reached over and put his hand on his friend's shoulder. "As long as you understand that, I think you'll be fine."

"It's a lot to take in," Brad admitted. "Even for us, it's a lot to take in. It's a process we're all working through, and it won't be perfect; it may never be perfect."

And that was the one thing Jared was afraid of. Not that it wouldn't be perfect, but that it would never be the same as it was.

SHELL HEARD THE door to the women's restroom open and glanced up, seeing Hannah. "Hey, I'll be fine in just a few minutes." She wiped at her eyes, trying to hide the evidence of the tears she was letting flow.

"Take your time." Hannah walked up and down the bathroom, checking under the stalls. "Because you and I are going to have a little talk." When she was sure they were alone, she turned back towards the door and flipped the lock.

"What the hell are you doing?" Shell asked, shocked.

"Hopefully helping you." Hannah folded her arms over her chest. "I'm gonna be real honest with you. Can you handle that?"

The old Shell? Fuck yeah; she could handle anything Hannah wanted to throw at her. This one? The one who felt like she was on the edge of a nervous breakdown, she wasn't so sure. "I think so."

"I completely understand what Garrett said to you in the car, but I'm telling you, I've been where Jared is. He needs you to meet him halfway. He needs your help, he needs you to be willing to take his clues and help ease him through the transition."

"What transition?" Shell asked, pushing her hair back from her face as she wiped her nose with a tissue.

"His whole life has changed."

She argued. "So has mine."

"Stop making this all about you and how hurt you are." Hannah glared at her. "You are welcome to your feelings, but so is he. It's your job, as the person he loves and who loves him back, to take his clues and help him where you can."

Shell didn't get it.

"He sat next to you, hoping to open up the line of communication, and you were so deep in your own head that you couldn't do anything but freak out when his leg touched yours under the table."

"How did you know that?"

Hannah snorted. "Because I know you. Whether you realize it or not, I probably know you better than you know yourself. Stop getting in your own way and stop holding back on what the two of you can have."

Shell wanted so badly to tell her friend that she was wrong, that she was looking too deeply into this. In the end, though? Shell knew she was right.

Squaring her shoulders, she walked back out and sat down next to Jared, having as pleasant of a meal as the two of them could have together. They went out of their way to be polite with one another, and when the checks came, he was a gentleman, picking hers up too.

Breathing a sigh of relief as they made their way out to the vehicles, Shell knew she was home free. Grabbing

EJ's carrier, she sat it on the base and then went to pull herself into the Land Rover. Jared's hand on her shoulder stopped her short. He held his hand out to her, and she looked up, their eyes meeting.

"Come to a meeting with me?" he asked softly.

"When?" Was out of her mouth before she could stop it.

"I'm headed there now."

The decision was there, but she couldn't make it. Not until she heard Hannah's soft voice from beside her, and she grabbed the carrier from the opposite side of the car. "Go, we got this."

For the first time in months, Shell put her hand in Jared's and trusted that he wouldn't lead her in the wrong direction.

# Chapter Eight

J ARED BREATHED DEEPLY to give himself a sense of calm. Obviously, Shell had never ridden on the back of a bike before, or she had and it had scared her shitless, because she was holding onto him so tightly he could barely breathe. It was nice, though, having her this close without her running away. He'd given her his helmet. No matter what, she was his first priority.

"You okay?" he asked over his shoulder, wanting to make sure before he started it up.

The other guys in the band had left, leaving them here by themselves. There was no other way for her to get home unless she called a cab. He prayed she wouldn't snap out of whatever this was and do just that.

"Yeah." She nodded, but her fingers dug almost painfully into his stomach.

He could handle it though—at least she was willing to be around him. "Alright, then let's go." He backed the bike up and turned them onto the street, heading towards the designated spot for this meeting.

A part of him wanted to open the bike up, the way

he liked to, just to see what Shell would do. The more sensible part of him knew that if he did, it might make her run. He had to play this safe and cautious. Already he was questioning why he had invited her to this particular meeting. It wasn't like the one he'd attended the other day. The one the other day focused on speakers; this one was more intimate and focused on sharing feelings on a particular subject. The damage was done now, and he would be damned if he backed out. If he wanted them to have a life together, she would have to accept him how he came.

SHELL WAS SCARED to death as she watched the buildings of downtown Nashville whirl past them. It felt like they were going a hundred miles an hour, but she knew it wasn't that fast. There wasn't enough room between stoplights for him to open the bike up like that, but it was fast enough to get her blood pumping. She dug her fingers into his stomach, holding on with everything she had and gripping the seat with her thighs. It was exhilarating, scary, and at the same time, she loved it. Much like her relationship with Jared.

They pulled into the parking lot of a church, and she wanted to question what they were doing there, but she knew this was all Jared's show. She had no idea how these things worked, and she was counting on him to let her into this part of his life. They parked, and he turned off the bike.

They were a tangle of arms and legs as she figured

out how to get off the contraption, breathing a sigh of relief when she was on solid ground again. Patiently she waited while he took the helmet off her head.

"Was it fun?" He ran his fingers through her hair, trying to tame the wild strands.

She wanted to curl into him and let him pet her hair for hours. The touch was enough to bring her to her knees, but she refrained. "It was different." She used her own hand to fix the other side of her hair. "But I liked it. Maybe next time not so fast?"

Had she really just said *maybe next time*? She hadn't meant to do that, but she wouldn't say no if he asked her.

He laughed. "We were going all of forty miles an hour, sweetheart. Just wait until I get you out on 65."

She turned her head to where she knew I-65 ran around the city, her eyes bugging. "That place is dangerous in a car, much less on a bike. Maybe we can stick to backroads for a bit?"

He wasn't about to look a gift horse in the mouth, so he nodded in agreement. "Will do. You ready?" He indicated the building with a nod of his head.

"Yeah."

There was no hesitation in her voice. She was ready for this. The part of her that held back was the part of her that wanted to know everything he went through. The truth—not some watered-down version of things meant to make him seem less damaged than he was. With him extending that hand into his real life, it had lifted the doubt off of her. He wanted to share this, then she would share it, but they still had a way to go.

Grabbing her hand, he pulled her with him to the entrance. She tried not to remember how much she'd missed that calloused palm in hers, but she had. She'd missed it a whole hell of a lot.

JARED'S KNEE BOUNCED up and down as he had a seat in the circle next to Shell. This was a meeting that a lot of significant others came to. That was one of the reasons he'd invited her. He wanted her to see they could have a relationship, even with him struggling sometimes. Chances were, he wouldn't even get an opportunity to speak at this meeting, but he wanted her to listen to the ones who did.

Just having her near was worth it. Smelling her shampoo and feeling the heat of her next to him energized him in a way he couldn't explain. He would probably never be able to if someone asked him. She gave him the will to want to live, to want to be better. Even when he'd been in rehab and refused to accept her calls or visits. It had been about him, not about her. He hadn't been ready to show her that side of him yet, and he hadn't wanted to scare her away. It was about self-preservation; not punishment.

"It's good to have everybody here tonight."

Jared's head snapped to attention as the leader started the group. They went through their normal beginning, reciting sayings and the Serenity Prayer before he opened up the floor. "How's everybody doing this week?"

Over to his right, Jared heard the voice of someone.

"Not great. I've had a rough week." He glanced over, seeing the face of a guy he'd seen in these meetings a lot. This crowd tended to run together in almost every meeting he went to.

He watched the guy glance over at the woman who sat next to him. "I was having bad cravings, and I pushed her away. We got into a huge argument. I went out and scored, and brought it home."

"But he didn't do it," the woman was quick to finish, grabbing hold of the man's hand. "He called me home from work. When I got there he had it laid out on the kitchen counter—perfect rows of white powder—and he was staring at it."

"I could taste it," the guy continued. "I knew the feeling it would give me, and my mouth was watering for it. I wanted to forget everything I was feeling, and I knew doing that one row, that one line, would fix everything." He reached over and grabbed her hand. "But when I saw her, I knew it wouldn't. I knew it would set us back. I could see the disappointment in her eyes, and knew if I did that line, this might be the time she wouldn't come back to me. I needed her, but at the same time, I wanted to push her away."

They glanced at each other, both teary-eyed, and Jared knew exactly how the guy felt. Needing someone that much was scary. Pushing them away was the easy thing, pulling them to you and letting them see all your vulnerabilities laid out on your kitchen counter was the hardest thing to do in the world.

He inhaled deeply when Shell reached over and entwined her fingers with his. His eyes met hers, and he could see the understanding there. Maybe inviting her to this meeting hadn't been the wrong thing to do after all.

# Chapter Nine

JARED PULLED THE bike up to the craftsman bunga-
low that had once belonged to Hannah and now
belonged to Shell. He shut the bike off in the driveway,
not sure what he should do. They got off—easier this
time because she'd figured it out.

"Thanks for coming with me tonight," he told her,
leaning against the bike. There was no way she'd be
inviting him inside, and he was good with that, but he
wanted her to know how much this had meant to him.

"Thanks for inviting me, J."

*J.* She hadn't called him that in a long time. That had
been their thing. No one else had known about it. It
made a smile spread across his face, and he wanted to
scoop her up in his arms. He didn't know if he could, he
didn't know if she would appreciate it, if she would even
allow it.

"It's important for me to have you see what I've
gone through." He put his thumb up to his mouth and
bit the nail. A nervous gesture he'd picked up when he'd
put the drugs down. "I hope after hearing that person's

story tonight, you kind of have a better idea as to why I didn't want to see you when I was in rehab."

"I do." She nodded. "But that still doesn't take away the pain and the hurt I felt every time you rejected me. Even if you didn't mean for it to be a rejection—that's how I took it. It fucking hurt, J. I wanted to crawl in a hole and never come out."

He wanted to say something but got the impression he shouldn't. Instead, he let her continue.

"I wondered what was wrong with me."

"Nothing," he answered immediately. "It was all me, sweetheart. All me."

She walked closer to him. "But that's where you start to question yourself when the person you love doesn't speak to you, doesn't even acknowledge your presence. You wonder what the fuck you did to make their feelings change."

He was frustrated. Grabbing her by the waist, he stilled her movements, anchoring her in front of him. "None of my fucking feelings changed. I am more in love with you today than I was then, because you haven't given up on me. You might want to ignore me, and you might want to punish me, but that's okay. I deserve that."

"You do," she threw back at him. "And what if I did give up on you?"

"You haven't, babe, because if you had, you wouldn't have gone to that meeting with me tonight. You wouldn't have come to rehearsal with Hannah today, and you sure as fuck wouldn't be here with me right now."

He took a chance, reaching out to caress her cheek. "I think you want to give up on me, but you can't, and it pisses you off."

She closed her eyes, tilting into the caress. "You hurt me more than any other person in this world ever has. You killed my spirit. I lay in bed crying for days. How is that me, Jared? How is that me?"

"It's not you, and I don't ever want you to get that fucked up over me again."

She tried to pull away from him, but his grip on her was strong. Stronger than it had been months ago. He was stronger. "That's easy for you to say, when you don't love me nearly as much as I love you."

There it was—the accusation she'd wanted to make for months. It slipped out in a moment of anger—like everything did with the two of them. They had to stop this.

"Aww, baby, is that what you really think?"

He looked gutted that she'd accused him of that. His face turned into a mask of misery, his eyes showing pain like she'd never seen before.

"I'm always a secret, Jared. I've never met your family."

"You have," he interrupted her. "The guys and Garrett's parents. They are my family. They're the ones who matter, and while we're on the subject, I've never met yours either. Hell, you *never* talk about them.

"I don't have any family." She shrugged. "Hannah is my family, and that's my choice. Our stories aren't that different." She dug into her brain, trying to figure out the way to say what she wanted to. She grasped for words and phrases and finally something came out. "But loving me means that you'll show me all parts of you, not only the good, but the bad too."

"You've seen the bad," he reminded her.

"Even then, you tried to push me away. Relationships aren't perfect," she reminded him. "They are messy and dramatic, while at the same time loving and stable. If you only give me one piece of yourself, you don't love me like I love you. I give you my flaws and all. You get the bitch, you get the emotional, and you get the whiny brat."

He pulled away from her and walked over to her garage where he leaned against the siding, crossing his arms over his chest. "I'm scared to give you all of me. What if you realize you don't love everything that comes with me, and you're gone? If you're really and truly gone, then I'm done. I have nothing to live for."

There it was, the truth she'd wanted to hear. Admitting that if she left, he wouldn't be anything—that was the closest he'd come to admitting how he felt about her, ever. She would take it.

Launching herself into his arms, she grabbed him around the waist and held on tightly, burying her head in his chest. "I love you, Jared, and there is nothing in this word that would make me leave like that. I saw the worst the night I thought you died. You weren't breathing." She cried, tears leaving her eyes for the first time. "Garrett was screaming at you to breath, sticking his fingers down your throat. He was losing it, and the whole time I stood there, telling myself you were dead. I was trying to figure out how I was going to live the rest of my life without you. What was I going to tell EJ about the man his uncle was? How was I going to explain to Hannah or the guys what I'd let you do to yourself?" That confession was ripped from her, her voice pained.

"No, babe." He grabbed her by the shoulders and forced her to meet him head on. "You didn't let me do that to myself. There was no way anyone could have stopped me. What happened that night wasn't your fault, and if you're carrying that guilt around—stop it now. I'm sorry you've felt this way."

Suddenly a huge weight lifted off her shoulders. Knowing he didn't blame her was one of the most freeing things she'd ever felt in her life. She hadn't realized how heavy that weight was.

Her voice was strong when she spoke again. "I love you, and I'm going to be here when you need me. I understand you might need to test that out, and you can, but know that I won't stand for bullshit. You're gonna be fucking honest with me, because that's what people who love each other do."

"It's not going to be easy with me," he warned her, cupping her neck in his hands. "I'm not an easy man to love."

She laughed, throwing her head back. "Tell me something I don't know."

His face got serious, and he moved his thumb up to her bottom lip, brushing his rough skin against her smoothness. "I love you. I don't think you know I love you. I'm gonna prove it to you. I moved here to get out of the craziness of California and to be closer to you. I'm gonna prove it," he vowed again. "The guys are here so that it's easier for Hannah and Garrett to live life—we're doing things we swore we'd never do so that everyone can be happy. I'm gonna prove to you that we can be happy too."

Wait, he'd moved here? That she didn't know, but she didn't have time to question it as he tilted his head to the side and leaned in, catching her lips with his.

She moaned as he tilted her head to make room for his. This was something she'd missed more than she could put into words. She'd never had a man before who kissed as good as Jared did. He threw everything he had into it. His body pressed against hers, turning them around so that her back was against the garage. She felt him put his free arm up against the wall, boxing her in. When he shoved his thigh between her legs, she thought she would fucking swoon.

Jared coaxed her lips open, pushing his tongue slowly against the roof of her mouth, tangling them together. He had to tell himself to slow this down and not make it into more than it was, but he'd missed her. Every single part of him had missed her. Their noses touched, and he pressed her harder into the wall when he felt her hands scramble up his back, pushing his jacket and shirt up with it. Cold air hit his skin, but it was welcome. It jolted and cooled him down.

Pulling back, both breathing heavily, he broke the kiss before giving her two more light ones.

His voice was low, strained, as he spoke. "You should go inside."

Looking at her, he knew she didn't want to, but they both recognized that it would be the smart thing to do.

"When will I see you again?" she asked, a dazed look on her face.

"Soon. I'll text you." The promise was there, and he hoped she took it.

Nodding, she pulled herself away from the garage and made her way up to the front door. Looking back one last time, she let herself into the house, giving him a wave.

When she shut the door, Jared couldn't wipe the smile off his face. Things were going to be okay—for once, he could feel it.

# Chapter Ten

**"I**'M ABOUT TO drink my weight in this stuff."

Shell giggled as she and Hannah had a seat at a local coffee shop. This meeting wasn't about business—it was about two friends meeting to catch up on life.

"Sleepless night?" she asked.

Hannah nodded. "Garrett knew I was coming with you today, so we made an agreement that I would get up with EJ last night, since he's gonna have him most of the day today. I plan on this coffee taking at least three to four hours." She took a sip of her cold concoction, sighing.

"Motherhood getting to you?" It had been a while since the two of them had met for an afternoon together. Both of their lives had changed—Hannah's obviously more drastically than Shell's had, but it was hard for them to get together for anything other than business.

"I love it," Hannah started.

"I hear a *but* in there."

She ducked her head in a way that almost made it seem as if she didn't want to be truthful. "When we talked about having a child, I don't think either of us realized the time that takes. I think we realized the work, ya know, but not the time."

"What do you mean?" Shell knew she wasn't the only one with problems, the only one who had things to talk out. They were friends, and that meant being there for each other.

"It's not as clear-cut as it once was. It used to be if Garrett and I wanted to go out to dinner, we spent twenty minutes getting ready, and out we went." She smiled at the memory. "Now, we have to get ourselves and EJ ready. Sometimes we call mom or you to come watch him—that adds more time. Then we have to make sure we have everything he might need or want while we're out. After that, we have to figure out if it's a place that'll frown upon us having a baby with us. It's a lot to think about."

Shell watched her friend, could see there was something else there. Her cheeks were red and she was squirming. Hannah obviously wanted to say something else, but she was either too embarrassed or it was too personal. "What?" Shell asked. "Tell me, or I'm not going to tell you what happened between me and Jared the other night."

"Okay, okay. Do you know what else sucks?" She pushed her hair back off her face. "I can't believe I'm going to tell you this."

"Well, you haven't yet, so get to tellin'."

She put her hands up to her face and took a dep breath. "So before we had EJ, we could have sex whenever we felt like it." She groaned. "Now it's planned, it's not spontaneous anymore—for the most part—and sometimes we're both so tired. I've fallen asleep twice during, and Garrett's fallen asleep once. How awful is that?"

Shell giggled, putting her hands up to her mouth to hold in the loudest outbursts. "You and Garrett?" she heaved. "Fell asleep??" She threw her head back laughing.

"You just wait until it's your turn. EJ may be a perfect baby ninety-five percent of the time, but that other five percent? He's a hellion. You should hear what Garrett calls him."

Shell wiped tears of laughter from her eyes. "Oh, this I gotta hear."

She leaned forward like she was going to divulge a huge secret to her friend. "He says EJ is cock-blocking him."

Shell dissolved into a fit of giggles again. "Oh Jesus, Hannah. I needed this. Thank you so much!"

She huffed and leaned back against the chair, folding her arms over her chest. "And these," she indicated her chest, "are never going to go back to normal."

"They will." Shell reached over and grabbed her friend's hand. "You're only a few months out from having him. It's going to take some time."

"Have I mentioned that the three times we've fallen asleep are the *only* times we've tried to have sex since I had him? In the beginning, I was scared, because, dude, my incision hurt. I mean it felt like something was ripping me in half if I moved the wrong way." She shook her head. "Then it was like Garrett was scared he was going to hurt me, or he saw me in a different way. Like I was no longer Hannah, I was Mom now too, and I've worried that maybe I'm not as sexy as I used to be. Now, since I've had EJ, I know I'm not taking the time to look cute, and it's all just ugh!"

Shell stopped laughing and seriously looked at her friend. "You mean to tell me that EJ is almost three months old—and you guys haven't done the deed since he was born? Not even on Valentine's Day?"

Hannah took a healthy drink of her coffee. "We haven't. Valentine's was more us just getting out by ourselves. We hadn't been out by ourselves together since he was born. Ya know the guys are going to Asia in two weeks. Who's to say Garrett's not going to find a *happy ending* over there?"

Shell did her best to hold in the snort that threatened to escape. It wasn't very often that Hannah got *this* worked up over anything—not anymore. "Okay, here's what you're gonna do…" Her brain was already working overtime.

"Pick a day, any day you want. I'll come watch EJ for a few hours, because I'm not going to kid myself into thinking you'll leave him overnight. You go fuck your husband's brains out. Don't tell him, just kidnap him."

Hannah sighed. "God, I love you. There was no way I could ask my mom to come watch him. She would want to know where I was going, and I just couldn't tell her."

"That's what friends are for." Shell waved off the praise. "Besides, I kinda like that kid. He makes me laugh."

The smile that lit up Hannah's face was large. "He is totally a joy to my life, and I'm glad we decided to go ahead and take the step. There's nothing that warms my heart more than watching Garrett and even Havock with him, but I still want to be Hannah, Garrett's wife, not Hannah, EJ's mom. Does that make me awful?"

"No, it makes you a completely normal person, and I'm honestly glad we're having this conversation. I've always said you need to take care of not only your physical well-being, but your mental too. Garrett is a huge part of that, and you're not one person—you're a lot of things to a lot of different people. So thank you for coming and being a friend to me today."

Hannah snorted. "Some friend I am. I've monopolized the entire conversation."

"No, you needed someone to talk to, and that's what I'm here for," Shell assured her. "I don't mind at all to listen to you. You're living a completely different life than I am right now, but I enjoy living vicariously through you."

Shell was quiet for a few minutes, not sure where she wanted to start. There were so many feelings she had about Jared, they all ran together sometimes and were not clear. It was hard to pick through and get the most important things out.

"We kissed last night," she blurted.

Hannah spit out the drink she'd just taken. "You did what?"

# Chapter Eleven

THAT WASN'T EXACTLY how Shell had figured she would tell Hannah the events of the previous night, but it'd come out that way.

"We kissed last night," she said again, wondering if she wanted to get into this, with her, right now. Part of her realized she probably should have thought this out a bit more, but there was another part of her that was so excited the situation had happened that she wanted desperately to tell her best friend about it.

"Okay." Hannah threw her hands up in the air. "Go back to the beginning. What happened after you left the restaurant with him—on the back of a friggin' motorcycle, might I add?"

She grinned, thinking about being on the back of the bike, holding on tightly to his waist. She could still smell the earthy tone of the leather, the spice of his cologne. Her fingers could still feel the hard edges of his ab muscles, the way they'd tightened as they leaned into a curve. The way he'd chuckled when she'd grabbed on a little too tight. "I wasn't sure what was going to happen, to be honest. When I grabbed his hand, all I knew was he was asking me to trust him, and for some reason I wanted to. I had no idea where we were going, where he would take me, or anything like that. I trusted him more in that moment than I've trusted him in months.

"Did you end up going?" Hannah seemed more excited than she had been, but Shell also knew Hannah had lived through this with her. She'd shared tears and excitement and sorrow. They had been in this together for so long that it felt weird for her not to share.

Shell had agonized over whether she wanted to truly tell Hannah where they had gone and what they'd done. It seemed so private, so intimate, but Hannah had been there for her through the whole thing. In a weird way, she felt like Hannah was just as close to the situation as she was. "Yeah, I went to the meeting."

"You did?" Hannah asked, and then it dawned on her. "Oh my gosh, he took you to a meeting? That's huge! Shell, people who go to meetings don't take that lightly. If they take you and include you in that part of their recovery, that means something. Jared is more intense than most. If he took you…" She shook her head, not able to come up with the right words. "He wants you."

She had tried not to look that deep into it, but hearing Hannah confirm how big it was made her stomach seize. The butterflies there were enough to make her light-headed. It wasn't the type of nervousness that accompanied the feeling that something bad would happen. It was the type that accompanied new love, and that's what this felt like. She felt like a teenager with a powerful crush. "I know, it was. I can't believe he took me. I've wanted him to make me a part of his recovery for so long, and I'm in shock that he actually did it. It was intense. And I don't know if he'll take me to more, but I hope that he does."

"Are you going to ask him?"

She'd thought about that. More than once. She still wasn't sure how she felt about the situation. Asking seemed almost like begging to her, and she'd told herself that she wasn't going to beg him again. That made her more vulnerable than she wanted to be when it came to Jared Winston. "I don't know. I feel like that's something he has to offer to do. If I start pressuring him, it might have the opposite effect, and that's not what I want to do at all. I'm thankful he thought of taking me, and I have to be happy with what he wants to include me in."

Hannah's eyes were wide as she continued to question. "What did you think about it?"

"I don't know," Shell was slow to answer. "I'm kind of still trying to process it. Jared didn't talk or anything, but one couple did, and what they said hit so close to home that he actually reached over and grabbed my hand. I haven't felt that connected to him in months."

"I think it's a good step that he wanted to include you and asked you to come. For someone like him, it's a vulnerability thing. He opens himself up, and then there's a chance he can be hurt that much worse. He's making progress, and he's including you in it."

Shell felt that pressure, and that's what it was—

pressure not to disappoint him, and even more pressure not to give up on him. Loving someone like him—those pressures came with the territory. "I know, and I never felt odd. No one looked at me or him like we shouldn't be there. He didn't try to hide me behind him; he let me stand directly beside him and face it head on, just like he did. I can't even begin to tell you why it meant so much, but it did." Shell grinned.

"About the kiss." Hannah grinned back at her, her eyes sparking with happiness for her friend. "You know that's what my sex-starved mind wants to know about."

"I'm not even sure how we got on the conversation, but we were facing off in the driveway, halfway talking, halfway arguing, and he's telling me he loves me…"

Hannah squealed, literally bouncing in her seat. If there was one thing Hannah Thompson was, it was a hopeless romantic, and she wanted everyone who knew her to be as in love as she was. "Oh my gosh, Shell. You had, like, the best night last night. This is what you've dreamed of. This is what you've wanted for so long. He's opening up to you. It might be slower than what you had envisioned, but I think he's going to get there."

Shell did too, but she was too afraid to say it out loud. "I know." She took a drink of her own coffee. "Like I said, I have no idea how we even got on the subject, but he tells me that I don't know he loves me, and he knows he's hard to love. He's apologizing for it, and he's telling me he knows he hasn't made life for us easy."

"That's the understatement of the year," Hannah

deadpanned, thinking back to everything the group of them had been through with Jared. None of them had been immune, and Shell had lived more than the rest of them. "No matter what he's been through, he does owe you an apology for how he's treated you."

"He kind of gave me that last night. We both agree he's not a man of many words, but they were flowing last night. And then, when I'm not even expecting it, he grabs me and kisses me."

Hannah sighed dreamily. "How was it? That was the first time you've kissed in close to six or seven months. Was it everything you'd hoped it would be?"

Shell thought back to the way Jared had owned her mouth, to the way he'd restrained himself in a way made even sexier because she knew just how wild he could be. She could still feel his fingers in her hair, his lips on hers. If she closed her eyes, she could see the look on his face; see the hunger in his eyes. Had it been everything she hoped it would be? That was a great question.

"Yeah." She grinned, biting her lip to try and hold the smile in check. "It really was."

# Chapter Twelve

"THEY LOOK GOOD up there."

Shell had to agree with Hannah's words. Black Friday did look good onstage together. Rehearsal was still in full swing for the band, and they were trying to lock everything tight before they had to leave in a week for Asia.

"They do. Way more put together than they were a week ago. They're hitting their stride." The week before, they were running into each other, Garrett's voice had been rusty, and some of the notes were a little flat. Now they sounded like a band. She knew once they had a show under their belt, they would sound like the normal Black Friday.

Shell watched as Hannah leaned down and adjusted the pacifier in EJ's mouth before she sat back up and faced her friend. "Are you going?"

"Going where?" Shell asked, confused as to what her friend was asking her.

"On the Asian tour? It's only two weeks, but I'm scared to take him overseas as young as he is." She motioned down to her son, asleep in his carrier. "Garrett agreed with me, so we're staying here."

The truth of the matter was, she didn't know. "I haven't talked to Jared about it, and I have some demos to do, assignments to turn in. Will it be fun? Probably, but I don't know if it's for me, this time."

Hannah folded her arms over her chest, glancing at her friend.

"What?" Shell felt as if she were about to be interrogated, and immediately, red flags were raised. "What now?"

Pursing her lips together, Hannah leaned closer to her friend. "Were you serious about what you said the other day over coffee? That you would keep EJ for a few hours."

A small smile played over Shell's face, and she grabbed her friend's arm. "Oh my God, you want a booty call with your hubby!"

"Shhhh! Shut up! If you'll watch him, I'm surprising Garrett." Hannah shushed her friend, putting her hand over her mouth.

Shell grinned evilly at her friend. It felt so good to be this way with her again, happy and carefree. The last few months had been one of the most serious situations she'd ever gone through, and because of that, these conversations had always had a serious tone to them. "You know I don't mind. When?"

She flashed the smile that had an audience eating out of her hand. "Would tonight be too short of a notice?"

"No, but I do have to let you know, Jared will be

there."

"Oh," Hannah deflated. "I don't want to interrupt the two of you. I'll do it another night."

"I don't mind, Han, really. It's not like Jared and I will be doing what you and Garrett are doing. I'm telling you because I don't know how you feel about him being around EJ. It's something we've never really talked about, and since I don't know every conversation you and Garrett have—I don't know what you're thoughts on that are."

EJ squirmed in his sleep, kicking his blanket off. Hannah bent over, fixing it again. "Neither one of us have a problem as long as he's with someone else. Obviously we wouldn't leave EJ alone with him—not right now. That's not to say that we won't ever. I believe Jared can get and keep himself together. Garrett does too. So yes, we'd be fine with him being there."

"Okay, then if you're good, I'm good. You want me to just take him home with me? That way you can leave and go get all pretty?"

Her eyes brightened. "Garrett and I did bring separate cars."

Shell reached down into her purse, fishing out her keys. "Why don't you take mine? I'll take yours, and Garrett can meet you at home. That way you don't have to switch out the car seat. I'm sure you have everything he could ever need in his diaper bag, and it's only for a few hours."

Hannah almost squealed with happiness. She reached over and grabbed Shell up in a hug before leaning down and kissing EJ on the cheek. "I know he'll be okay with you."

"He will. You know I'm not gonna let anything happen to him."

Up on stage, the group had finished the song they had been playing and looked to be taking a break. Shell watched as Hannah grabbed up her stuff and all but ran over to where Garrett talked to one of the guitar techs. She leaned in, tapping him on the shoulder. He gave her his full attention as she leaned up on tiptoe and spoke in his ear.

Shell waved when his gaze swiveled over to her, throwing him a huge grin. He grinned back before he wrapped his arms around Hannah and lifted her off the ground.

"What are those two smiling about?"

She glanced up, seeing Jared standing over her. "We're doing a little babysitting tonight. Seems like the two of them need to get reacquainted. Is that okay with you?" she asked, scared now that he might not want to have anything to do with EJ just yet. She definitely wanted to see him tonight, so she hoped she hadn't been presumptuous.

"I have no problem with it, but what do they say? Are they okay with letting me be around him like that?"

Shell could see the look in his eyes, could see that he worried they wouldn't trust him. It did her heart good to know that she could tell him it would be fine.

"They're good with it, as long as I'm around, and I will be. I wanted to make sure you're good with it."

He had a seat beside her, reaching down to grasp EJ's little hand in his. "I haven't gotten to spend much time with this little guy. There's nothing I'm looking forward to more than doing just that with you."

When he turned his smile on EJ, her heart melted, her ovaries exploded, and she damn near told him that she forgave him for everything he'd ever done. But her brain knew it wasn't that easy and they still had things to talk about.

"Then I'll definitely see you tonight?"

Jared nodded. "I'll just follow you from here and grab some food on the way."

She agreed and leaned her head back against the couch she sat on. If she closed her eyes and wished hard enough—she could imagine this was their child, they were married, and this was their reality. One she hoped they would have some day. If they could stick it out, this was exactly where she wanted to be.

# Chapter Thirteen

"**H**OW OFTEN HAVE you watched him?" Jared asked, amazed at how comfortable EJ was with Shell. He eyed the two of them as she changed his diaper. She had already fed and burped him.

"Not too often." She shrugged. "But I've been around him almost since the day he was born. He's used to me, and it helps that he's a good baby." She finished changing his diaper and then snapped the legs of the onesie he wore. "He's got a full stomach, he's clean, and I guarantee you, if I put him in the rocker over there," she pointed to an automatic rocking swing, "he'll be out like a light."

"You do all this like it's second nature to you." He couldn't get over how efficient she was.

"I helped Han out after she had him. She had a c-section, and it was hard for her to lift and move. Garrett still had things to do with the record company, and a few times I spent the night at the house with her and EJ. Instead of waking her up when he'd cry at night, I figured out how to do it. Really, he's been patient with me, and in turn taught me patience." She put him in the rocker and turned it on. For a few minutes, she stood over him, making sure he was comfortable and he wouldn't have trouble going to sleep. "And he's out." She grinned.

"Now we can eat?" Jared asked.

"Yeah, and don't worry about being quiet. That kid can sleep through a tornado. He's gonna be a good baby to have on the bus—whenever that happens."

The two of them went to the counter that doubled as a breakfast bar and opened the food Jared had brought. "I hope this stuff is still your favorite," he mumbled under his breath.

She opened the bag, smelling the Chef's Special from a local Mexican restaurant as well as jalapeno dip that she loved. "Oh my God, I haven't had this stuff in so long."

Shell didn't tell him it was because the two of them had gone there so often. It hurt to walk through the door and know he wasn't there with her, that he wouldn't join her for dinner.

"I haven't either." He took the lid off his food and inhaled deeply. "Even when I moved back here, I couldn't bring myself to go without you. It was kinda always our place."

"Ditto." She smiled over at him, thankful he got it. Thankful that for once they were on the same page.

They sat across from one another, both wrapped up in eating their dinner and thoughts crowding their minds.

"Can I tell you something?" he asked, taking a drink of the water bottle in front of him.

She glanced at him, noticing for not the first time how good he looked. Sobriety and taking care of himself looked good on him. She prayed harder than she'd ever prayed for anything that he would keep this up. She couldn't handle getting hurt again. "You can tell me anything."

He set his fork down softly. "I'm scared to go on tour."

Shell was floored. Jared was hardly scared of anything. Even facing down death, he hadn't been scared. "Why?"

He pushed his container away, running a hand through his hair. "I don't know who I am on tour anymore. Here, in Nashville, where I'm at home, I have a routine. I know where I can go, what I can do, who I can hang out with. On tour, it's different. You know that." He blew out a frustrated breath. "There are temptations—especially in the part of the world we're going to. I'd be stupid not to already be thinking about it."

"I'm not here to tell you that things are going to be easy." She looked him straight in the eye. "The old Shell, the one who hadn't seen her boyfriend almost die, might have told you how strong you are and how you would never let something like that influence your recovery."

Crossing his arms, Jared leaned back against his chair, listening to her. "But what would this Shell say?"

"This Shell cares about you as much as the old Shell did, but I have to tell you this. You have to want to be clean, you have to want to stay sober—and you have to work the program. If you don't, then all the time you've put in doesn't mean anything." She took a deep breath and pushed her own food away. "I'm not sure I can handle you going off the deep end again, either."

"That's it, that's my fear," he told her softly. "When I get into that headspace, where all I want to do is use, I don't recognize right from wrong, good from bad. Consequences mean shit to me, and I don't want to lose you. I know I don't have you back yet…"

"You don't," Shell confirmed. "I'm still not sure what to do with you and what I can live with. I wish I could give you something more concrete than that, but I can't. I'm willing to spend time with you; I'm willing to do anything that I have to, to help you. But," she bit her lip, "I can't do it all, and I won't be your punching bag—verbally or spiritually."

"I don't want you to be." He reached over and grabbed her hand. "I don't deserve a second chance. Fuck, I don't deserve to even be sitting here with you right now, but you're the only person I can tell this shit to."

A part of her heart, the part that hadn't been broken, fluttered when he admitted that. The other part of her heart, the one that had broken and was still healing, told the fluttering feeling to fuck off. "I want to hear this, I do, but I can't watch you go down that path again."

He rubbed his thumb along her knuckles. "God help me, Shell, I don't plan to."

# Chapter Fourteen

"I'M NOT A bad mom for wanting this. Right?" Hannah spoke to her reflection as she examined her body in the mirror.

She wore a tank top and a pair of shorts that showed just the curve of her ass cheeks. Anticipation was killing her as she waited for Garrett to get to the house. He'd texted her almost thirty minutes ago telling her that he was leaving the rehearsal space.

Closing her eyes, she took a deep breath. "You're not a bad mom for this."

She felt stupid talking to herself, but she didn't want to interrupt Shell, because she'd already done that by asking her to watch her son. Texting Stacey was out of the question, she didn't want to talk to her sister-in-law about her brother in the carnal way, and there wasn't anyone else she trusted. Instead, she squared her shoulders and leaned down, running a hand over her leg. Yup, smooth as it was twenty minutes ago when she'd gotten out of the shower.

"C'mon, Garrett." She tapped her dark-colored fingernails against the granite countertop of their bathroom. Just when she was about to give up, she heard the garage door open and Havock's excited barking.

Not sure how she should greet her husband after all this time, her heart sped up in her chest. Should she be on the bed? Should she meet him on the stairs? Should she not do anything? Months of not having the time to touch him were getting to her. She'd never been this unsure in her life.

Her contemplation was taken out of her hands when the door to the bedroom opened and they faced one another. Sexual tension was as thick as it had ever been, and Hannah didn't know what to do.

"Hi." She waved, a smile on her face.

That's when Garrett took off the sunglasses he'd wore all the way up the stairs. And by the look in his eye, she knew she was in trouble. He strode towards her with a purpose, grabbing her by the ass and picking her up so that her legs circled his waist.

GARRETT COULD BARELY see through the haze of sexual need as he felt her cling to him for dear life. All he knew was that he'd walked in the bedroom, and there had been his wife, standing there like a wet dream, wearing a white tank top and white shorts that were almost indecent. Gone were all the thoughts that had kept him from doing this before. He didn't have one ear open, listening for EJ. He wasn't worried about hurting her incision.

His only concern?

Getting his cock inside of her in the next two minutes.

Burying his hands in her hair, he tilted her mouth so that he could take possession of her lips. Those lips could bring him to his knees when they wrapped around his length, turning him on as she deep-throated him, or when she said something sassy when he wasn't expecting it.

"Fuck, Han, I've missed you." He pulled back, moving the edge of the tank top down so that her breasts were exposed to his eyes. With one hand, he lifted the globe up this mouth, using his tongue to circle the hard flesh, nipping lightly as she moaned against him. "I've missed this."

"I missed you and this too." She clung to him like he was a life raft in the middle of a tumultuous ocean.

In a way, that's what he felt like. His body wasn't his own anymore. It was now ruled by lust and his dick. Walking her over to the bed, he laid them down, not letting go of her flesh. His head moved this way and that as he sucked on the nub, using his teeth to inflict a bit of pain with her pleasure before soothing it with his tongue.

She pushed up against him, grinding herself against the tent in his jeans. "I can't wait, Garrett. The first time doesn't have to be perfect."

He pulled away, gazing into her eyes. "There will be more than once?"

"Oh yeah, Shell's got him for a few hours. As wet as I am right now—this first time may only take a few minutes."

LARAMIE BRISCOE

Garrett was on the verge of arguing that he'd be lucky to get his cock completely inside of her before he embarrassed himself, but they were married, and they were doing this together. Smashing their lips back together, he moaned, thrusting his hips towards her.

Her hands fought with his, releasing his belt buckle and pushing his jeans down his legs. With one fist, he grasped his shirt and pulled it over his head, wanting to feel her skin against his. Leaning back in, he made a circle around her other nipple with his tongue. Trying to lift it deeper into his mouth, his fingers kept getting caught in the fabric of the tank top.

"Fucking thing," he cursed as he ripped it straight down the middle, finally exposing her body like he wanted to. Next up were her shorts, and when he had trouble with those, he ripped them too. Leaving her naked to his eyes.

"You're the most beautiful woman I've ever seen," he told her, running a hand along her stomach.

"Even with stretch marks?" she asked in such a way that said she was joking, but he could tell by the very serious look in her eyes that she meant it.

"Those stretch marks turned us into a family. There's nothin' more beautiful than that."

She didn't have time to respond. He sunk his length inside of her, causing both of them to moan loudly. His thumb moved to the center of her body, strumming against her as he found a shaky rhythm.

"I wasn't kidding, babe. Forgive me this time." He thrust inside of her, withdrew, thrust again, and groaned deeply as he found his pleasure.

"Me too, almost there." Hannah breathed deeply against him through her nose as he latched onto her neck, thrusting through his orgasm.

The last thing she expected him to do was withdraw completely and enter her with two fingers, keeping his thumb on her clit. He worked her, entering, withdrawing, and strumming. On the third sequence, he felt her body tighten, and her nails dug into his forearm, holding him tightly against her.

Both of them panted as they lay back against the pillows.

"Now that that's out of the way," Garrett grinned over at her, "we can really get down to business."

She shrieked as he captured her flesh in his mouth again, thrusting himself against her. She grinned. This had been the best idea Shell had ever had.

# Chapter Fifteen

"I HAVEN'T WATCHED this since you left," Shell admitted, with a smirk on her face "It scares me to watch it by myself."

Jared laughed. *The First 48* had kind of been their thing. That and any crime show they could find. It wasn't unheard of for them to marathon an entire season of *SVU* in a weekend. "You always were a bit of a scared Susan."

"This shit is real-life," she protested, sitting up straighter on the couch.

"It is." He nodded. "That's what makes it so interesting."

"No." She shook her head. "That's what makes it so fucking scary."

He opened his arms wider for her, and she did what she'd wanted to do all night—sink into them. It by no means meant that things were perfect, and they both knew it was a learning process. Tonight, she wanted to feel protected. She didn't want to have to keep up appearances. Tonight, she didn't want to hold onto her anger.

Closing her eyes, Shell sank back into his arms, letting this transport her to a different time. The time before she knew what he looked like fighting for his life, the time when she didn't question if he loved her or not, the time where all that mattered was sneaking off together. It didn't mean AA/NA meetings or trying to hide her heart.

Leaning her head back against his chest, she let herself sink into the fantasy.

JARED TRIED TO concentrate on the show that played on TV, but he couldn't. All he could think about was the woman in his arms, the smell of her shampoo in his nose, the perfect way she tucked under his chin. Back before his OD, he'd taken this for fucking granted—he hadn't know how long it would be before she was lying against his chest, re-claiming her spot. He'd never take that shit for granted again.

He stretched his legs out on the couch, getting comfortable with her soft body against his hard one.

"We'll be able to hear him, won't we?" He hitched his chin in direction of EJ.

She laughed. "Oh yeah, little man's got a nice set of lungs on him. We'll hear him, don't worry about that."

They lapsed into silence, and Jared let his mind wander. Immediately his thoughts went back to when he was in rehab, and he would lie in bed at night—that was the worst time. He missed the guys, he missed playing his guitar, but mostly he missed her. Closing his eyes, he could see the smile on her face, the love in every expression she gave him. He tried not to think about the pain and fear the last time they had been together at the club. It didn't do anything besides make him wish he'd been a better man.

Reaching down, he grabbed her hand in his, stroking her palm and using his finger to write her notes. He hadn't done this since high school, and even then it'd only been to try and get in the girl's pants. *Hi*, he wrote with the tip of his finger.

"Hi." She giggled back to him.

Thrilled that she got the game, he smiled to himself. *You're hot.*

"So are you." She turned so that she lay on her side, able to see his face.

He stopped the game for a second. There was something that had been weighing on his mind, and he had to ask her. In reality, he knew he had no right, but it was something he had to know.

"I'm a bastard for asking you this, but it's something that's bothered me." This had, the entire time he'd been in rehab and pushing her away. He'd had to do that for himself though. For once Jared had to concentrate on Jared, in a very health way.

Accommodating as ever, she looked into his eyes, so fucking trusting. "I'll answer whatever you need me to. Anything to help."

"Was there anybody else? Did I push you away that hard?" The question was asked softly. He immediately felt her stiffen and wanted to punch himself in the face. "No, you don't have to answer that."

"I will because you asked, but I honestly can't believe you asked me this. Is your self-esteem that shot, because I never took you for someone who needed this kind of reassurance." Her eyes flashed an irritated glare at him.

"We all have our fucking hang-ups."

She closed her eyes and counted to five, calming herself down. "Since I met you, there's been no one else but you. You'll never have to know how I feel sharing you with something else."

He situated himself back on the couch, feeling more comfortable in his skin. "Thank you, not only for being faithful to me, but for the honesty too."

Shell turned her attention back to the TV, and he could tell by the set of her shoulders that he'd irritated her. He couldn't help it though; there were things he had to know. She let him grab her hand back, and he used his fingertip to make a few more words.

Turning around, she grinned up at him. "Lord, I don't know what I'm going to do with you, but I love you too. Take this slow with me, and please don't hurt me again." Her feelings were plain as day on her face—along with the fear.

They both knew he couldn't make promises he might not be able to keep. "We'll take this slow."

She flopped back against his chest, an exasperated sigh escaping her lips. He wrapped his arms around her neck and pulled her close. He was right where he wanted to be, right where he needed to be, and he hoped like hell he didn't fuck this up.

"HE WAS REALLY good," Shell told Garrett as she helped him get EJ strapped into his carrier a few hours later.

Jared had just gone home, and Garrett had texted her to let her know he was coming to get his son.

"I'm glad. Thank you again for watching him." He leaned in and gave her a hug.

She hugged him back. "You're welcome. He's a good baby; I don't mind at all. If you two ever want a night alone again, just let me know."

A blush washed over his face, and she couldn't believe it.

"Stop blushing in my house and get the fuck home to your wife."

He laughed, flashing his dimples at her. "I'm about to, but while I got you alone. How was Jared?"

She'd waited for this. Garrett was as concerned for his friend as the rest of them. "He did great. I think this time he might actually kick this habit."

"I want to believe that." Garrett ran a hand over his chin, scratching the new growth of whiskers. "But it's going to take more than a few months for me."

"He's gonna have to prove it the rest of his life," Shell answered quietly. "But we have to make sure we don't stifle him because we're worried he'll relapse."

"You're right." EJ shifted in his carrier, making a face in his sleep. "I better get him home. Thank you again."

"No problem." Shell saw them to the door and watched as Garrett strapped EJ in the Land Rover and they pulled out of the driveway.

Alone again. The story of her life lately. Things, however, seemed to be looking up.

# Chapter Sixteen

"**H**ERE'S SOMETHING ELSE we got at the fan page."
Shell handed Hannah a piece of paper she'd
printed out from Facebook. "It's talking about a charity
auction for a little kid with cancer. I've done some
research on it, and it's legit. They're asking for you to
donate some stuff. We have those old tour shirts, and I
think there's some old programs too. You could sign
them, and I could mail them off for you."

Hannah was reading over the piece of paper as she
fed EJ, who sat in her lap. "My God, I don't know what
I would do if something happened to him. This breaks
my heart," she said as she read over the request.

"I know." Shell sighed. "My thoughts immediately
went to EJ, which is why I thought you would want to
help."

"Yeah, most definitely. See what you can get from
the warehouse, and I'll be more than happy to sign it."

Shell grabbed her folder and looked through it.
"That's all that we have that's pressing right now. Next
week we may need to go into the office; there are a few

contracts that have been presented. You'll want the legal team to look over those, though."

"Sounds good," Hannah said as she grabbed a cloth and wiped up EJ's mouth. "You done?" she cooed to him as she moved the bottle from his mouth and picked him up to begin burping him. "So have you decided what you're going to do about Asia?" she asked as she patted his back.

Shell put her stuff back in her bag and turned to face the mother/son duo. "I've decided not to. I really want to, but I don't want to be the only girl there. Stacey's not going, and you're staying here. Jared and I are still kind of weird with one another, and I'd need support dealing with him."

"What about the support he needs dealing with the tour?" Hannah fired back.

"Don't go all mama bear on me about Jared. He's my problem, not yours."

Hannah wrinkled her nose. "If you think he's a problem, then *that's* a problem. He's not; he's a human-being who's trying to make his life better."

*Shit.* "I didn't mean it like that. I truly didn't. Now you're putting words in my mouth and making assumptions."

"Look, I'm going to be honest with you." Hannah finished burping EJ and set him back down in his carrier, handing him a toy to play with. "He's still very vulnerable."

"You think I don't know that? He's not the first person I've loved that's had an issue like this." Shell was getting sick of Hannah talking like she didn't understand the importance of the situation. "I'm vulnerable too. Just because he's the one who decided to end it all, doesn't mean my feelings don't matter."

"I know, and you're right, but you have to be mindful of the words you speak. That's all I'm saying."

Shell counted to herself, trying to calm down. That's how she'd made it through the past few months. Counting to herself when she seriously wanted to lay into people. "I will, but I won't let him walk all over me."

"I'm not asking you to," Hannah reiterated.

"As long as we understand each other."

"We do," Hannah agreed.

"WHAT BRINGS YOU here today, Jared?" his sponsor asked. Malcolm was a man he'd met on his second day in Nashville, and he'd been a savoir. When things got to be too much, he could call Malcolm and he would meet him. No matter the time, no matter the place. It was nice to be a priority in someone's life. Today that time was seven o'clock in the morning at a park in the heart of Nashville.

"I leave for Asia tomorrow." He took a drag off the cigarette he held in his hand. "It's my first time on the road since rehab, and Shell's not coming with me."

Malcolm whistled between his teeth. "That's scaring you?"

"Fucking terrifies me." He threw his cigarette down and got up, snuffing it out with his shoe then pacing.

"We've been to Asia before. I clearly remember the things I did over there the first time. They treat us like Gods over there—the only place they worship us more is fucking Brazil. Anything we ask for, they give us. There isn't one person who will say 'no'."

"And you need that?"

"Yes, I need someone to hold me accountable, someone to tell me no when I'm being an asshole. I need someone to call me on my shit and help me be grounded. That person is Shell. I'm kind of pissed that she decided not to come with us."

Malcolm nodded. "Now we're getting somewhere. Why are you pissed?"

Jared was quiet for a few minutes as he worked through his thoughts. Really worked through them and tried to figure out what the fuck he was trying to say. "I'm pissed because she's strong enough to not let me control every aspect of her life. It used to be, if I asked her to come, she'd move hell and earth to do that. I ruined it."

"Or maybe she just got stronger and realized you're the one in charge of your own recovery. What she does only affects a small portion of how you feel about yourself. She can only support you so far, Jared. The rest has to come from you."

Jared knew Malcolm was speaking the truth, but it wasn't easy to hear. "I don't want to let her down again. I don't want to let the guys down again."

"Do you want to let yourself down?" Malcolm asked the hard question, as always.

That was it. Did he think that much of himself? He was so used to saying that he didn't. Punishing himself was so much easier than trying something and failing. "No." He shook his head. "I don't want to let myself down either. I'm worth more than I've been putting into myself."

"Then I think you'll do just fine, Jared. Remember the big picture here—the rest of your life, Shell, touring, EJ. All of that hinges on the choices you make."

Jared hoped like hell he could continue to make the right ones.

# Chapter Seventeen

D RIVING TOGETHER TO see Jared and Garrett off wasn't something Shell ever thought she would be doing with Hannah. Back when the two couples had gotten together, she'd assumed that wherever the boys went, they would go too. That was before Garrett and Hannah got married, before EJ was born, and before Jared had gone to rehab. So many things had changed in the past couple of years—it was enough to make her head spin, and while she wasn't looking forward to this, she knew she was strong enough to deal with it.

"You ready?" she asked Hannah as she glanced over at her friend.

Hannah was doing her best to keep it together, but Shell could see she was upset. Purposely, Jared had come to pick Garrett up that morning so that the two ladies could ride with each other while the guys hopped their plane heading to Asia.

"As I'll ever be. This is harder with EJ than I ever imagined. It's only two weeks, but I'm scared to death something is going to happen," she admitted.

"That's why I told you I'll stay with you for as long as you want me to. It's not a big deal. All I have in the next few weeks are some demo dates, some stuff for you, and online courses. Any of that can be done at your house, just like it can be done at mine," Shell reassured her.

"Thank you for being here."

Shell snorted as they got out of the Land Rover. "I could tell you the same thing. Helping you will help me not go insane wondering what the fuck Jared's doing. I'm as nervous as you are."

"He'll be fine. This is his chance to prove to anyone who bothers to look and listen that he's good. I think he knows how much this means, and I don't think he's gonna let you or the guys down."

"I'm more worried about him letting himself down," Shell told her as the two of them walked into the airport.

Sometimes it was a blessing to live in Music City and to be a well-known band or recording artist. It meant you got access to special lounges where you could wait before your plane boarded. For once, Shell was glad she wouldn't have to do a goodbye in front of people. This one was more emotional than any one she'd ever had before.

As SHE WALKED into the lounge, holding the door open for Hannah, who carried EJ in his carrier, Shell's eyes immediately met Jared's. She'd never seen such a scared expression on his face in her life. Not caring who saw, she raced over to him, throwing her arms around his waist. She buried her nose in his neck and held on for dear life.

Shell was aware of him walking them somewhere, but she had no idea where until she pulled her head from his shoulder. He'd moved them into a room off to the side so that they could have some privacy.

Unexpected tears hit her full force, and she didn't bother hiding them from him as they streaked down her face.

"Oh baby, please don't cry. Please, you're killin' me," he rasped as he leaned in and kissed her softly on the lips.

It hit her all at once, and she did her best to hold in the sobs, holding her body tight and still. "I'm scared for you."

"God, Shell." He threaded his fingers through her hair, pulling her close to him, dwarfing her body with his. "I'm scared for me too, but I don't want you to worry. That's the last thing I want you to do. This is going to be okay."

"How do we know?" Her voice muffled against his shirt.

"We don't," he admitted. "But I've been given tools, and I've got a lot to come back to here. I'm sick of disappointing you."

"I'm sick of the disappointment." She hadn't meant to say those words, but they were true, and she meant them. Maybe it was time to say them. She fisted her hands in his shirt, pulling him closer to her. "Don't do it to me again."

"I wish I could tell you it's never going to happen again, but I don't know the future. I don't the situations I'm going to be put in. I can promise you that I'll try not to be dickhead or be stupid." He put his chin on her shoulder. "I wish you were coming with me."

This was too deep a conversation to be having at an airport, but they were who they were, and conversations came when they did—no matter where they were. "I can't always be your fallback; you have to prove to yourself that you can do this without me."

A frustrated noise erupted from deep in his throat. "I've *been* doing it on my own. That's why I didn't want to see you in rehab. I wanted to prove to you that I wasn't using you. I wanted to prove that I didn't always have to be a fuck up, but all I did was succeed in pushing you away." His voice was hoarse as he continued. "I didn't mean to; fuck, I didn't mean to. You took it in a way you weren't supposed to."

Fresh tears erupted from her eyes, and she pulled back from him so that she could see his dark eyes. It was important for her to see if he was being honest. When she gazed into his eyes, there was nothing but sincerity there. Finally, Jared was laying his feelings out on the line—the way she'd wanted him to for so long. "You're going to be fine. You need help, you call me. I'll be there, no matter what time it is. We've got to prove to each other we can do this. It sucks, but J, this is real life." She cupped his face in the palm of her hands, feeling the scrape of the beard that was growing in. "Real life isn't always going to be perfect, and we get through it however we can. I love you, and I think you can do this."

He closed his eyes, feeling the words she said, happy as fuck she'd told him she loved him. "I love you too, and I'm going to do this for us."

"No." She grabbed his hand, holding it to her chest. "You do this for yourself. I'll be here, and you can do something for me later, but you do this for you and your band. They need reassurance as much as I do."

This time, he wasn't going to let anyone down. He leaned in, giving her a kiss that promised that, not only to her, but to himself too.

# Chapter Eighteen

"**I** HATE THAT I'm going to leave you here with him. I wish we had thought about what could possibly be going on in our lives when we made this schedule," Garrett told his wife softly, holding EJ in his arms.

"Life happens, and we can't always plan for all the unknowns. It's roughly two weeks. We'll be fine," she reassured him. "Shell said she'd stay if I need her to, and don't forget my mom and dad are in town."

Garrett glanced at her, his eyes showing a bright green through his glasses. "He's going to grow and change so much in the time I'm gone. I hate that I'm going to miss it."

"This is our job," she reminded him, putting her hand on his shoulder. "We've gotta do what we've gotta do to keep a roof over our head and food on our table. Some parents work a nine to five; we work a crazy schedule for a year, and then we're off for a year. We'll make this work. He's not going to forget who his daddy is."

She wrapped her arms around the both of them, giving them the tightest hug that she dared.

"You don't forget who your husband is either," he spoke deeply in her ear. "It's been a long time since we've not been with each other."

She tried to think back to when that was, and it hit her; right after they were newly married and she'd been forced to do a crazy number of shows in a small amount of time in order to appease the record label. That had been a stressful period in their lives, and she was glad it was over.

"It won't be like it was the last time," Hannah promised, leaning up to kiss him on the neck. "We're much better prepared than we were last time, and how in the world do you think I'm going to forget who my husband is? I love you in the crazy, scary, *I'd find you* way," She giggled. "Seriously, this is going to be okay."

He shifted EJ back down to his carrier, grinning as Brad came over and grabbed it. "Here, I'll watch Little Man for a few minutes."

"How weird is this role reversal?" Garrett grabbed her around the waist now that he didn't have to worry about his son and pulled her close. "Usually it's me telling you that everything is going to be fine. I'm the one telling you not to freak and calming your insecurities. I'm not used to all this shit."

She giggled into his shirt. "It's okay, babe. I got you."

He groaned, hearing her speak the words to him that he normally spoke to her. "Just like I got you." He leaned in, capturing her lips with his. Garrett was mindful of where they were and the fact that they couldn't let anything get out of control, but they were who they were. He reached down and grabbed her hips, pulling her fully to him. "Damn, I'm gonna miss you."

"Ditto," she answered, pulling away from him. There was regret in her eyes, and for once she wished they'd planned EJ's birth better. She wanted to be with her husband, and it was going to hurt seeing him take a plane without her.

"Guys," Rick said as he entered the room. "It's time."

The mood was somber as everyone said their good-byes to one another—each band member taking a minute to say bye to EJ.

"Love you." Garrett leaned in, kissing Hannah one more time before getting EJ on the cheek. He looked at Shell. "Take care of my family while I'm gone."

"You know I will. They'll be good." She reached in and gave him a hug.

Jared grabbed her hand. "Y'all be safe."

She giggled, trying to keep from crying. "Funny how you've easily slipped into Southern vernacular."

Feeling cheeky, he flashed her a heart-stopping smile. "I could very easily slip into something else Southern, but I don't think we're there yet."

Shell was speechless as Hannah sputtered next to her.

"I love you," he told her, reaching in to run a finger along her chin.

Before she could answer, he was gone.

Shell and Hannah watched their retreating backs for

as long as they could, until they could no longer see them walking down the hallway towards the security check for their gate.

"C'mon." Shell put her arm around her friend. "Let's go home and do one of two things. Binge watch something hilarious, like *The Big Bang Theory*, or find some gelato fast."

Hannah laughed, wiping at her eyes. "Just know this, Michelle," she said in a mock-stern voice. "This girl does not Netflix and chill with anyone besides Reaper of Black Friday."

Shell threw back her head, laughing so hard she also had tears come to her eyes. "Thanks," she sniffed. "I needed that."

"You're here for us." She nodded down to EJ. "We'll be here for you."

She knew without a doubt that in order to be strong for Jared, she would definitely need her family to be strong for her.

# Chapter Nineteen

*Hong Kong*

GETTING USED TO the time change was a major bitch, but Jared knew he had to keep his schedule. If he didn't, he knew his chances of staying clean weren't as great as they could be. Stumbling out of his bed, he blinked bleary eyes before grabbing his phone. The time read four in the afternoon, which meant it was two in the morning at home. No wonder he was so fucking tired. They'd gotten in the night before, or maybe it had been early morning, he couldn't remember. One of their planes had been delayed and it'd thrown them completely off.

Rummaging around in his bag, he grabbed a pair of running shorts and a tank top. This wasn't some place he was familiar with, so he knew the best place for him to be was the hotel gym. He texted Garrett.

*Wanna work out?*

While he waited for his friend's answer, he went

about brushing his teeth and trying to wake himself the fuck up. He'd never been the type of person to wake up early. Hell, even on benders, he'd stayed up instead of going to sleep and waking up at weird hours.

*Give me five, I'll meet you downstairs.*

That made him feel better, knowing that Garrett would be there with him. It was accountability and friendship. Two things he hadn't been sure he'd feel with Garrett again. Grabbing his stuff, he made his way to the elevator and downstairs to the gym.

He got there before Garrett, which he'd figured he would do. Taking a minute before he started his warmup, he checked his messages to see if Shell had sent him anything.

*Hey, just wanted to let you know, I'm thinking about you. You'll be fine, I know you will...and if you need anything, I'm always here on the other end of the phone line.*

Jared couldn't help the grin that covered his face. He was a lucky bastard and he knew it, because if their roles were reversed, he wasn't sure he would be as understanding as she her.

*Thanks! I'm about to work out with Garrett. I'll give you a call later.*

Putting his phone in his pocket, he looked up as Garrett came through the door. To say he was nervous was an understatement—the two of them hadn't really talked since he'd been back from rehab. If any opinion held the same weight Shell's did, it was Garrett's.

THEY FOUND TWO treadmills beside one another that weren't occupied, and both started their warm-up. Jared focused on breathing deeply—in and out—as his legs ate up what would be miles. He kept thinking about how he wanted to approach the subject of his recovery with Garrett, but nothing sounded right.

"How are you doing?" Garrett finally asked after they had been warming up for a few minutes.

"I'm good," Jared answered, his voice strong, breathing controlled. "But then again, we haven't been tested yet. Or at least I haven't been tested yet."

"You gonna pass that test when it comes?" Garrett asked.

Jared glanced over at his friend and saw that Reaper was in full effect. His eyes were hard, his expression closed off.

"I deserve that."

"You deserve that and a whole lot more."

Jared took a deep breath. "So this is it? We're gonna have it out finally?"

"We haven't had it out yet," Garrett reminded him. "We've been kind of polite around each other. Probably to a fault."

Jared understood what he was saying and he also knew that it was time to put a stop to it. "Let me have it." He continued running, staying in his zone. If he was going to take it like a man, he knew he would have to do it where he was comfortable. The only place lately he was comfortable, besides on stage, was with Shell or working out.

Garrett opened and closed his mouth. "Dude, I don't know if it'll do any good. What if it sets you back?"

"Do you think I gave a fuck about *you* when I was getting high? I mean, seriously. It's time to give me as good as I gave. I can take it, Reaper. Come at me." Jared squared his shoulders, ready to take whatever verbal assault his friend would unleash.

GARRETT HAD NEVER quite felt a black anger wash over him like this one did. So often, he tried to keep the Reaper part of his personality in check. He tried to keep his anger to himself and not let anyone else privy to it, but this time, he knew he had to let it out. He had to let it fly, and he had to trust that Jared could handle it.

"I'm so fucking pissed at you, and I do mean that in present tense. I'm still fucking pissed."

His voice was deceptively quiet, but he kept it that way so that they wouldn't draw attention. There were a few other people besides them working out.

"The thing is, I don't know what I'm pissed at the most. I don't know if I'm pissed because you did what you did to me, you broke Shell's heart, or the fact that I almost had to tell my son who his uncle Jared is through pictures and a visit to your grave."

Jared flinched when Garrett said those words, and Garrett took note of it.

"Yeah, motherfucker, at your grave. Do you know how close you were? Do you know how that felt? Putting my fingers down your throat so that you'd throw that shit up." He stopped running but noticed that Jared didn't and that was fine; Jared had to get through this, however he could. That he could respect.

"Shell was scared to death when she called me, and I immediately knew it was bad. I don't know how, but I knew it. I broke every speeding law there was getting to you, and then I saw how gray you were. She was crying, and my dad was trying to hold it together, and I knew I had to take charge. Do you know how hard that was?" He stopped and took a deep breath.

"I have a son, you asshole. A son that I want you to know; I want you to be a part of his life, because you're my best friend. You, Jared, more than anyone, molded who I was as a kid and a teenager, because we've always been each other's right hand…when mine was gone? Fuck that shit, man."

"I'm sorry," Jared told him.

"Fuck the 'you're sorry'. Make a change and make it stick. I am not going to raise my son showing him pictures of his uncle and telling him what a kick-ass dude you are if we have to visit you at a grave site. You got that? Not because of some stupid shit you did." Reaper continued on, stepping up onto the treadmill and putting himself close to Jared, so that he could hear him. "And I guarantee you, a ten like Shell, she won't stay single forever if you're a dumbass and throw it away. But above all, man, do it for you. You're worth it, Jared. Do you hear me?"

Jared faced forward, trying to control the emotions that were making his throat close. Garrett reached down, turning the treadmill off, and forced Jared to face him.

"You. Are. Worth. It."

Jared shook his head.

"No, fuck what people have said in the past. We want you here." Garrett's voice went hoarse. "I need you here. Who's gonna teach EJ about Pantera and Dimebag?"

Jared chuckled. "That's gotta be Uncle Jared."

"It does." Garrett nodded. "So make sure you stick around, huh?"

Jared heaved a sigh of relief. "Yeah, I'm gonna."

Garrett clapped their hands together and gave him a man hug. "You make sure that you do. You're loved, bro. You are fucking loved."

# Chapter Twenty

NERVOUS ENERGY COURSED through Jared's veins. It was the best kind of high, the *only* kind of high he would be getting from now on, if things worked out the way he was determined they would. He stood off on the side of the stage, going over in his mind the show they were about to play. His legs shook, his hands shook, and he felt like he was going to hyperventilate, but damn he'd missed this.

"You good?" Reaper asked as he came over. He was in full concert mode; the sunglasses and swagger were on.

"Yeah." Jared grinned, and he meant it. He hadn't felt this alive in such a long time. Even back over the summer, before his relapse and OD—things had felt off for him. It was something he couldn't explain, and he hadn't told anyone about it. How could you tell someone what you didn't know yourself? Now though, he felt like he could conquer the world.

"I can't wait to get out there with you, Train."

Train. It had been a million years since he'd heard

that name. He'd never again let it be that long because he'd been a dumbass. Seeing this through new eyes was making all the difference in the world.

AS SOON AS the curtain dropped and he saw the thousands of people who had packed the arena, he knew he was meant to be here. Everything he had been through, everything he had put the people in his life through was culminating in this.

Not missing a note was his goal, interacting with the crowd was his pleasure, and being on stage with his best friends? That was his life. They were nearing the end, and he was sweating like he'd run a 10K, breathing hard too, but it was the best kind of exhaustion he was feeling.

"So y'all know we had to cancel a few shows last year, and we had some personal stuff come up," Reaper was saying to the crowd. "One of the things that came up was my son." He smiled widely, and the crowd went insane as a family picture flashed on the screen.

Jared glanced up, smiling himself at the picture of Garrett, Harmony, EJ, and Havock. They really were the perfect family in his eyes. No, they didn't always have everything together, and sometimes they fought, sometimes Garrett made her cry, but he always apologized and they always worked it out. That's the kind of family he wanted, the kind of relationship he wanted to be in.

With a clarity he hadn't had in a very long time, he realized he *was* in that kind of relationship. He'd made

Shell cry; hell, he'd almost died on her, and she'd accepted him back, not with open arms, but she'd eventually let him somewhat in. They weren't perfect, they yelled at each other, and he knew there would be a lot more yelling before this was all said and done, but she hadn't left. She. Hadn't. Left.

Reaper was still talking. "The other thing that happened was our man Train over here got into some trouble. He's been in rehab, and we're standing beside him one hundred percent." The two of them faced one another, and Reaper put his arm around Train's shoulders. "He's gonna need everybody in here to think some good thoughts for him. This is his first night back on stage. He's gonna need a round of applause."

The force of the crowd clapping, whistling, and stomping their feet almost knocked Jared down. When they started chanting *Train* it was everything he could do not to emasculate himself and cry. The love that came from this group of strangers was like nothing he'd ever felt in his life.

Reaper came over, leaned down, and repeated the words from earlier. "You are worth it."

And damned if right now he didn't feel like he was.

"HOW WAS THE show?"

Jared smiled tiredly at Shell. "It was great, like nothing I've ever played before in my life. I wish you could have been here."

She smiled back at him, propping the phone up as

she continued getting ready. "I wish I could have been there too, but there's too much going on here."

"Where are you going again?" he asked as he lay down in bed and got comfortable. That long not touring always made him a little sore the night of the first show back and the next day.

"I have a few demos to work on, and then I have to go to the library and get some research done for a paper. Then I'll probably come back here and see what Hannah wants for dinner. She's napping right now because EJ's napping," she explained, putting mascara on her lashes.

"You lookin' all hot for someone?" he joked, but there was a little bit of true question in his voice.

She tilted up the side of her mouth. "Myself, and I thought maybe if this guy halfway around the world wasn't asleep when I got home, maybe we could FaceTime."

"Call that dude; he'll wake up for you. Not an issue."

Her eyes softened. "Seriously, I don't want you to wear yourself out."

"I won't," he promised. "I'm in better shape now than I've ever been, and to be honest," he ducked his head, licking his lips on purpose. He watched as her eyes followed his tongue. "I really fucking miss you."

She stopped what she was doing and picked up the phone so that she could concentrate on him. "I really fucking miss you too. By the way, I really like the stubble you've got goin' on. Maybe you could do that for me once you get stateside."

His dick hardened. A flirty Shell was a fucking hot

Shell. "You flirting with me?"

A bored grin on her face, she winked. "It's been a while, but I hope I haven't lost my touch."

"Nah, sweetheart, you still go it."

She smiled widely at him this time. "Then I'll be calling you later, but right now I really gotta go."

"Alright," he moaned. He wanted to talk to her all night and not think about any of the hundred guys that she would probably run across before he got to see her again. "Be careful, and have fun."

"I will." She tilted her head to the side. "You forget, I've been taking care of myself for a while now."

He copied her, tilting his own head. "Oh, I know, but I'm telling you right here and now, I want that job back."

He didn't give her a chance to refute or ask questions—he cut the signal and lay back, a satisfied smile on his face. That had felt amazing.

# Chapter Twenty-One

SINKING DEEP INTO his bunk on the bus, Jared sighed. They'd just played their sixth show of their twelve show tour. To say he was tired was an understatement; he still wasn't completely acclimated to the time change and figured he would get there the day they left.

He'd been a little more to himself this time than he'd been in previous tours, but part of that was because he was focusing more on his life. Usually they were all out partying together and staying up late, writing music. This time, Garrett was missing his family, Chris was focused on finishing his degree, Brad was constantly trying to talk to Stacey, and he was doing his best to keep his relationship with Shell going.

He checked the time. It was midnight where he was, meaning it was ten in the morning where she was. Deciding he had nothing better to do, he pressed a few buttons on the phone and waited for it to connect.

SHELL LAUGHED AS EJ splashed her. "Look, dude, I know you don't like bath time, but you've got to do it!"

As she reached over to grab the soap, her phone went off. Heart skipping a beat as she saw Jared's smiling face, she answered. "Hey!"

"Hey," he answered back.

She heard him. He looked tired, and his voice was hoarse. "You okay?"

"I'm good, just tired. You know how it is."

Shell did know; she could remember being so worn out with Hannah. It had been a while, but she could still feel the stress and the tiredness that had permeated her body. "You feelin' down tonight?"

He sighed. "Fucking exhausted. To be honest, I just want you here in bed next to me. That was something that always grounded me, no matter what. I need that grounding tonight," he admitted.

"Too bad for you, some other guy's got me." She winked, moving the phone over so that he could see EJ.

A smile spread across his face, and he moved a hand behind his head, showing his tattooed bicep. "How's he doing?"

"He misses his daddy. Anytime Hannah talks to Garrett on FaceTime, he sits there like it's the most amazing thing in the world. He watches he understands what's going on." She rolled her head on her shoulders. "He finally slept through the night last night for the first time since y'all left."

"Have you been getting up with him?"

She nodded as she continued scrubbing him down.

"Yeah, Hannah's got enough on her plate with worrying about Garrett being over there. There's some things the record company wants her to do too, so she's got a lot going on. I figure getting up with him during the night is the least I can do."

"Then why are you giving him a bath?"

"See," she laughed, "what happened was…I thought it'd be a good idea to give him some juice, and you know he's started to hold his stuff up pretty well. This bottle was a little heavy, and before I knew it, juice was every-where." She wrinkled her nose. "You know how sticky juice is?"

He laughed along with her, yawning. "I can't wait to get back home," he said quietly. "I need my routine."

"Are you having a hard time?" she asked, finishing up the bath for EJ and wrapping him up in a towel. Suddenly she felt scared, her nerves rattling.

"No," he answered, and it was the truth. They'd been too busy for him to have a hard time; plus he was as focused as he'd ever been. "I'm just ready to get home to you and work out in a place that's familiar. I never thought Nashville would be my home, but I've never felt more at home than I do there."

"That makes me really happy," she admitted, trying not to get her hopes up. Getting her hopes up with him hadn't always worked out, but she was willing to play it out—however it was going to. For once in her life, she wanted to have no regrets. She would see this through until the end, no matter where that took them.

He yawned again.

"Why don't you go to sleep? I'll talk to you later?"

"Only a few more days, and then I'll be home." The promise was in his voice and on his lips.

"I can't wait." And she couldn't. She felt like a piece of her was gone without him around. She'd had enough of that to last a lifetime.

They disconnected the call, and she wished with everything she had that he would be coming home the next day. This Jared, she could get used to.

# Chapter Twenty-Two

"ARE YOU SURE you don't want me to drive you to the airport?" Shell asked Hannah, trying her best to be polite.

For the first time ever, she really didn't want to. She wanted to have this time to herself with Jared, not have to worry about whether or not Hannah and EJ were taken care of. For once she wanted to be selfish and enjoy her time with her boyfriend.

"I'm sure." Hannah shifted EJ, putting him over her shoulder. "It's late, and Garrett doesn't want me getting out with EJ. You go and have a nice reunion with your boyfriend. We don't need the added stress of possible paparazzi. I'll be fine waiting for him to get here."

"I hate leaving you here." That much was true. As much as she didn't want to be responsible for Hannah and EJ, she hated that they were going to be at home while the rest of them would be with one another.

Hannah walked over and hugged Shell. "I thank you for what you've done for us the past few weeks, and I love you for it. Now go get your man."

Shell laughed, throwing her head back. "Yes, ma'am."

As SHELL PARKED at the airport, she pulled down the visor and checked her makeup. Tonight, she was excited that he was home. They'd left things so emotional, and sometimes it was hard to keep up the anger towards him. Many times in the past few weeks, Jared had done something to remind her that he hadn't always been an asshole. A sweet text or a nice phone call had reminded her of the letter he'd written her that Garrett had delivered, telling her he loved her. That was the Jared she wanted to remember—and tonight, the only Jared she wanted to remember.

Getting out of the car, she smoothed the hem of the sweater she wore over her jeans. Late March was still cool in Music City, and she'd paired a long sweater with jeans and riding boots. They came up over her calves, almost to her knees. Once, when she'd worn these with a dress, Jared had told her exactly how much he'd loved them. Her momma didn't raise a fool; she wanted his attention tonight.

*We just landed, they're getting our baggage and they're holding us in the same lounge we were in before. But I'm out back of that, smoking a cigarette.*

The text that came through from him made her heart race. Suddenly she was breathing as if she'd run a hundred-mile race. Making her way through the airport, she kept her head down, not wanting to see anyone she knew. Now wasn't the time for her to get stopped and asked about Harmony. She had a one-track mind, and that was to get to Jared as quickly as possible.

Rick stood outside of the lounge door and smiled widely at her. "You can go through that door." He pointed across the hallway. "It leads directly to where he is. That way you won't be waylaid by the guys."

"Thanks." She grinned over to him. "I'm beyond excited."

"He is too," Rick assured her.

She made her way over to the door as quickly as possible, pulling it open and stepping out onto the concrete. "Jared!"

His head had been bent over his phone, checking something as he took a drag off his cigarette. When he heard her voice, his head popped up, and a smile the likes of which she'd never seen spread across his face.

She took off at a run, squealing when he caught her.

THIS WAS THE welcome home he'd secretly wanted when he'd come back from rehab but knew he hadn't deserved. Pulling her legs up, he let her circle them around his waist as she wrapped her arms around his neck, holding on tightly.

"I missed the hell outta you," he told her, angling his head so that their lips could meet. The kiss was out of control before it even got started. He desperately needed something to lean against, because she was eating him up with her lips.

Jared let himself stumble, holding tight to her thighs until his back hit the hard surface of a wall. Once there, he let the structure take their weight and moved his hands up her thighs, past her ass, up under her sweater.

"Tonight." She gasped when his hands went further up her shirt and came around to the front to cover the silky material of her bra. "I don't want us to do what we're supposed to. I don't want it to be about what happened a few months ago." She moaned when he used his thumb and forefinger to tweak one of her nipples. "Tonight, I want to be Jared and Shell. I need to know we can still be that together."

He was right there with her, ready to make that dream a reality. There was nothing more he wanted than to show her a good time. It had been too long, and he was sick of rehashing things that weren't going to change. They could work on their relationship tomorrow after the sun rose. Tonight, he wanted to spend the darkness with her. He wanted her to be his light.

"Come home with me," he whispered, breath heaving as he pulled away from her lips. "Spend the night. Fuck everything we're supposed to do."

She gave him a saucy smile. "I'd rather you fuck me."

He pushed his hips against hers. "I'm right there with you, sweetheart. I am totally on board with that. What do you say?"

She thought for a minute, throwing caution to the wind. "I have my vehicle. Let's go."

Setting her down on shaky legs, he grabbed her hand.

They were crazy for doing this, and they both knew it. But love was sometimes crazy, and it didn't always make sense.

# Chapter Twenty-Three

SITTING IN THE passenger seat of her car wasn't something Shell did very often. Normally when she was in either her car or Hannah's, she was the one doing the driving. Tonight was very different. Jared sat in the driver's seat, navigating them through the late-night Nashville traffic. One of his hands sat on her thigh, the other one was wrapped firmly around the steering wheel.

She couldn't stop touching the hand on her thigh. Using her fingers, she stroked the palm, up and down, making circles, before moving on to his fingertips, feeling the callouses there. They were hard against her softness, causing goosebumps to break out along her entire body. She'd never known anyone's hands to turn her on this much, but she'd missed him—everything about him—and being near him tonight was dangerous to her libido.

"You keep doing that, and I seriously might come in my pants." His deep voice spoke from over the console.

Her head snapped up and her eyes met his. What she saw there was desire and blatant arousal. "Sorry." She cleared her throat, but she didn't drop his hand. A piece of her had to be touching a piece of him.

"Don't be sorry." He grasped her fingers with his. "I just wanted you to know, when we get to the house, this might not be the romantic night you've probably envisioned."

She took in the picture he made, her mouth slightly open as she fought for breath. His arm was stretched out, showing the sleeve tattoo he sported from shoulder to wrist. His forearm flexed as he engaged the turn signal and made a right turn, using the palm of his free hand to maneuver the steering wheel. When she watched his fingers slowly grasped that wheel and flex themselves, she felt it in between her legs. Shell wanted to laugh; she didn't even know why every movement he made was the biggest turn-on for her. Moving her gaze from his hands, she glanced at his face and had to smile. He was still sporting the tiny bit of stubble she'd told him during one of their FaceTime sessions she liked. If she were honest with herself, she couldn't wait to feel the rasp of that tiny bit of hair all over her body. It was time to be honest with Jared.

"I'm not envisioning romantic and slow." She pulled her bottom lip between her teeth. "I'm thinking hot, fast, race-to-the-finish-line, down-and-dirty sex like we haven't had in a long time."

*"Fuck,"* he moaned, grasping her hand tighter. "I'm thinking you've got it about right."

The two of them were quiet as he pulled into a parking garage. "You're living *here?*" she asked. It occurred to her that she'd never asked.

"Yeah," he laughed.

"Taylor Swift has a condo here." She eyed him. Of course she knew that together Garrett and Hannah had a lot of money, but funny how that had never come up with her and Jared. She'd always kind of assumed he'd squandered it.

"You think I don't have T. Swift money?"

She snorted. "I'm thinking that there are very few people who have that kind of money."

"You're right." He parked her SUV and handed her the keys. "I don't have that kind of money—my condo is a few floors below hers, but I love the building. And while I do waste money, embarrassingly, I have my own contracts for guitars, and I've been smart with some investments. I can take care of you, even if I do make questionable decisions sometimes."

"It never crossed my mind," she said as they got out and met each other around the front of the SUV.

"It's something I want you to know." He leaned in, giving her a kiss on the forehead. "You ready?" he asked as he nodded towards the elevator.

As she was ever going to be. "Yeah." She let the side of her mouth tilt up, giving him the kind of heart-stopping grin he hadn't seen in months. "I am."

So was he. God, so was he.

JARED MADE A concentrated effort to slow himself down and not attack her on the way to his condo. Wrapping her hand in his, he made sure to keep her at arm's length as he rolled his suitcase along behind them. Trying to play it cool, he fished his keys out of jeans pocket, and quickly unlocked the door. Pushing her in front of him, he used his foot to slam the door shut.

They faced each other, both quiet but breathing heavily. Arousal and sexual tension was high in the air, but both of them seemed scared to act on it.

"Remember what I said about the first time not being romantic?" he asked, moving his hand down the front of his jeans, cupping himself through the denim, showing her how hot he was for her.

"Yeah." Her hands went to her sweater, pulling it up over her head. "I'm completely down with that."

His fingers went to the button on her jeans, unclasping it as he pushed the material down around her hips, taking her panties with them. Grasping her up, he walked them into what she found out was the kitchen when she glanced around. She squealed when he sat her on the cold granite countertop and then went to work on his own jeans, pulling them down far enough to get his length past his zipper. "I'll make this up to you, I swear to God." He nipped at her earlobe, grasping it between his teeth.

"You have nothing to make up." She moaned, shoving her hands down the loosened back of his jeans, digging her fingers into his flesh. "I want this as much as you do." It was erotic, feeling the cotton of the shirt he wore against the nipples that rubbed the silk of her bra.

Jared pulled back, knowing he should take his time

with her, knowing she deserved better than this. He was worried, though, that if he gave her enough time to think, she'd be gone. He couldn't have that, not today, not right this minute; he fucking needed her. "Are you still protected?"

She shivered as his stubble scraped against her skin, leaving a trail of goosebumps in its wake. "Yeah."

That was all he needed to hear; he grasped his cock by the root, held it steady, and sank deeply into her. They both moaned uncontrollably as he did so. Jared was embarrassed to admit that he was almost there; just one thrust deep into her, and he was ready to come. Six months was a long time to go without the woman you loved, and he was feeling that right now. Using his thumb, he flicked against the hard nub of her clit, not stopping the thrusts in and out of her body. They were shallow now, not nearly as deep as they had been a few seconds ago. Sweat covered his forehead as he tried to keep his dignity about him, but he knew it was worthless. His legs shook with the effort.

"God." She tilted her head back, closing her eyes against the strong feelings that coursed through her body, thrusting up against his cock and his thumb. "Faster," she breathed, grasping the front of his shirt and yanking him towards her. She felt the scrape of his lip ring as he circled her nipple with his tongue.

Pulling back, he panted. "Much faster and I'm gonna have to pull out and make sure you get there first." He buried his head in her neck.

Hearing this man who was larger than life and such

an important part of her world be brought to his knees was all it took. She gasped, opening herself wider to him.

"I love you, Shell," he moaned, nipping at her neck as she felt him spill deeply inside of her.

Just like that it was over, and they took stock of where they were, giggling. She pushed his hair off his forehead. "I love you too," she whispered, before clearing her throat and speaking louder. "This doesn't make everything okay. You know that, right?"

He nodded, because he did. He hoped it hadn't fucked everything all up.

# Chapter Twenty-Four

SHELL WRINKLED HER nose as she loaded her dishes in the dishwasher. She was feeling off since she and Jared had seen each other the night before, and it wasn't just because of the quick sex. She'd expected that. She'd gone into it knowing that was exactly how it was probably going to go. What she regretted was that she hadn't asked him how things were going. They hadn't had a chance to talk about the tour. Being together had been more important.

Finishing up, she put soap in the dispenser and started the machine. Just as she was about to sit on her couch, there was a loud knock at the front door. She wasn't expecting anyone, but at least she looked decent.

Opening it up, she smiled as she saw Jared standing there.

"Hey!" She leaned up, hugging him around the neck. No awkwardness was a blessing. That had been one thing that worried her.

"Hey." He leaned in, giving her a chaste kiss on the lips. "You got plans?"

"Laundry." She pulled a face. "That I absolutely do not want to do."

"Come with me then." He reached out and grabbed her hand.

"Wait! Where are we going? I might need to change, and maybe fix my hair." She immediately put her hand up to her hair, trying to tame it.

He stopped pulling on her hand and turned so that he faced her, using his big palm to cup the entire side of her face. "You look just as beautiful right now as you did last night coming on my cock."

She laughed, her face burning red. "What a charmer you are!"

"I try."

"Really, where are we going?"

He leaned down so that they were more on each other's level. "I get my six-month coin tonight, and I'd like for you to be there. I know it's not much, and it feels like I'm rehashing shit I've already given you." He remembered giving her his old one the previous Valentine's Day. "But, I want you to be here for this. I want you to be as involved in this as you can. I don't want to hide anything from you."

She knew this was his way of including her in his process, and she had to be open to it. It wasn't easy for Jared to open himself up and invite people in. "Of course I'll be there. Do I need to bring anything?"

He shook his head. "Just yourself. I'm on the bike, so you might not even want to bring a purse. Anything you need, I got it."

She tried her best not to be flattered and impressed, but she was. This was the Jared she'd missed like hell. The one she hoped everyday would be the one who made it out of this.

THIS TIME, SITTING in the meeting beside Jared, Shell felt more comfortable to offer her hand. Even though things weren't perfect between them, she felt like she deserved to be here, and that she could be a part of his life without being a hindrance. That was a big thing for her.

"I see some new faces, some old faces, and some faces that I'm very proud of tonight," the meeting leader said as he glanced around the room. "Jared is getting his six-month sobriety chip tonight."

There was a round of applause, and Shell felt like she clapped louder than anyone else. She was that proud of him. She watched as the leader made his way over to Jared and gave it to him.

"Thanks." Jared looked down at the coin in his hand, and she wished she knew what he was thinking.

"You wanna say anything?"

Jared was quiet for long minutes, and Shell thought that maybe he'd sit this one out, not offer anything this time, but then his deep voice filled the silent room. "This isn't my first rodeo. Two other times in my life, I've sat in these meetings and gotten chips for being good at working the program. Once, I was even sober for a year."

"What's different this time?" Someone spoke up

from beside them, and she glanced over, seeing a young guy.

"This time, it's more than myself to think about." He grabbed Shell's hand and squeezed. "The woman sitting next to me has been to hell and back with me, and I owe it not only to her, but myself, to make sure this sticks."

The guy beside them spoke again. "My lady, she told me I had to do this, that in order for us to be together, I had to get my shit together."

Jared sat up straighter. "I'm gonna be real with you, brother…you look young."

"Twenty-two last week."

"Dude, you're a baby. You're gonna fail—it might not be my failure—which was fucking epic, but there will be something on this journey that takes you more than once to get. Don't give up on yourself. Don't let others give up on you. Give yourself permission to fall down, get up, and dust yourself off. You're gonna need that. Make sure you keep your friends and your girl close. If she's asking you to get help, man, she cares about you. Don't throw that shit back in her face," he advised the younger guy.

Shell couldn't believe what she was hearing. Her boyfriend—and that's what he was; he'd never stopped being the man in her life. The man who never said more than thirty words at one time was telling this kid how it was and what he could expect with the life of an addict. He wasn't sugar-coating it either.

"At some point, you're gonna fuck up, and you're gonna have to ask for her forgiveness again. If she doesn't give it to you, if your friends don't give it to you, you have to accept it. You accept it, you come back here, and you work the program. You get yourself a sponsor, and you work the fucking program. That's what it's here for, that's what we're here for. You're not alone."

The kid glanced up and recognition glowed in his eyes. "Thanks, Train."

He let go of Shell's hand, got up, and walked over to where the kid sat, putting his hand out. "There is no Train here. My name's Jared, and if you need something, just ask."

Shell had never been as proud of him as she was in this moment, and she fought against tears that threatened to fall. He was finally getting it.

# Chapter Twenty-Five

"ARE WE DOING anything with the band today?" Jared asked Garrett as the two of them ran in Centennial Park.

"Rick had said something, but then he said it was cancelled. As far as I know, our schedule is wide open for at least a week. Did you get the email that said we have to go back to California at the end of March for those meetings about the new record?" Garrett groaned. "I never thought I would say this, because you, of all people, know how much I love the ocean and my house, but this place feels so much more like home. I don't have to worry about people trying to get pictures of my family here, and it's less crowded."

"I totally agree with you, and I never thought I would say that either." Jared reached up and wiped the sweat off his face. "There's much less temptation here, and I don't always have to be *on*. Plus, I'm pretty sure Shell won't ever move out there for good."

"How are things going with her? I haven't wanted to be all up in your business, but I do hear her and Hannah talking every night, and man, the giggling the other night. What did you do?"

Jared flashed him a self-satisfied smile. "We kind of got reacquainted, if you know what I mean."

Garrett laughed. "I kinda figured. Hannah has this one giggle, usually it means she's talking about sex, and I knew it wasn't about me." He pursed his lips. "We're getting better, but we're still trying to figure out that part of our lives with EJ."

"You'll get there," Jared assured him. He had no fucking clue, but that's what you were supposed to do for friends. He forged on. "The reason I asked if we had anything going on today is because I think I wanna take Shell out. For like a day date. We haven't done that yet."

Their mile counter went off, and Garrett stopped, walking at a fast pace to start their cool-off. "You're serious this time, aren't you?"

Jared felt like he could be honest with his best friend. There had been times in his life when he hadn't been, but now was a good time to start. "I love this girl, I want her in my life for the long haul, but I know I've fucked this up—more than once. I'm trying to prove to her and to all of you that I'm serious this time. Unfortunately, I know that it's hard for all of you to believe it, so the important thing is I keep working until it clicks."

All the other times Jared had tried to get clean, he'd never taken responsibility for his own actions. They'd had numerous conversations like this—the two of them—and in the past, it had always been about how people had done him wrong. He blamed the guys, he blamed his parents, and he blamed his childhood. Garrett had never heard him own up to his own short-comings. "I'm proud of you." His voice was sincere, clear, and honest. "I've never heard you be this way before when it comes to your recovery. I have hope it'll stick this time."

Jared stopped walking and faced his friend head-on. "Before I left for rehab this time, I sat a table doing lines of Coke, and I had the distinct impression that if I don't take this seriously, if I don't make this stick and work the fucking program, I'm dead. I can't say for sure when that will be, but I had the feeling that if I don't kick this shit, I'm going to die, and it'll be sooner rather than later. Regardless of the bullshit I've spewed for years, I honestly don't want to die. I hope that immature Jared of the previous years is gone. I have shit to live for, which is way more than most people who battle this disease have."

Garrett could have dropped to his knees and cried. This was exactly what he'd preached every time he'd talked until he was blue in the face. Grabbing his friend up in a hug, Garrett closed his eyes. "You get it."

Jared hugged him back. "I do, I finally do."

SHELL FUSSED WITH her hair, trying desperately to get it to lay the way she wanted it to. Thirty minutes before, she'd gotten a text from Jared that told her to get ready; he was coming to spend the day with her.

She would have been lying if she hadn't said that her

stomach hadn't bubbled with anticipation and excitement. The fact that he wanted to spend time with her made her happy, it made her think he'd really changed. Before, he'd been so closed off to her that finding out how he felt was like pulling teeth, and while it wasn't *easy* now, she realized being with him and sharing moments was easy. There was a knock on her door, and she all but fucking skipped. *Calm down*, she told herself.

She opened the door and smiled slowly as she took in the picture standing in front of her. This man, her man, looked so good. Worn jeans hugged his thighs, a black T-shirt showed off the now flat stomach he sported, an equally worn leather jacket hugged his bigger biceps, and mirrored aviators along with black motorcycle boots made him look like the baddest of bad boys.

"Hey."

Had she sighed that word? Had she really sounded that desperate? The amusement on his face told her she had.

"Hey yourself." He took the sunglasses off.

Looking into his dark brown eyes, she again saw the amusement. "Stop."

He gave her an innocent look. "Stop what?"

Growing flustered, she opened the door wider so that he could come in. "You know you're hot. Just stop."

He laughed, crossing the threshold. "I love the way your eyes eat me up though. Makes me feel like I could take on an entire country on my own and beat the shit out of a world champion welter-weight."

She had no doubt he could do those things either.

"What are we doing today?"

"Spending the day together; we haven't done that enough." He walked over and wrapped her in his arms.

She inhaled the spicy scent that was him and rested her head on his chest. "Sounds good to me. Let's go!"

# Chapter Twenty-Six

SINCE JARED HAD never done the touristy things Nashville had to offer, Shell was excited when he parked in a garage off Broadway.

"I've never walked up and down Broadway or Printer's Alley or any of that hokey stuff," he told her, a smart-ass smile on his face as he said the word hokey.

"It isn't hokey, you asshole. This is part of the history of Nashville." She laughed as they got out of his truck.

March in Nashville was a crap-shoot. It could either be cold, with winter sticking around and even snow, or it could be nice, with spring making an emergence. Luckily for them, spring was making an emergence. Grabbing her jacket and his hand, she directed them out of the parking garage, and they randomly began walking.

Up and down the city streets, they walked, talked, and window shopped. As they made a turn, Jared stopped them by pulling on her hand.

"Has Hannah ever played here?"

She saw they stood in front of the Ryman. "She has." Shell smiled, remembering that night. "It was early in her career, before the Bridgestone or even the Woods at Fontanel came calling. I have to tell you though; I'd rather her play a venue like this than the arena. When they say that's the church of music, they aren't lying. You walk in that place, and you can feel it."

"I'd love to play there," he admitted. "An all-acoustic show, Reaper and Harmony. Damn, could you imagine it? Their voices meld so well together, you singing back up, me playing an acoustic guitar. I'm gettin' chills thinking about it."

"Why don't you tell them?" Shell looked up at him. "Not everything is about Reaper and Harmony, ya know? There are other people involved too, and I bet they would be all for it. I'm not kidding when I tell you it's one of the most amazing venues in the world that we've ever been in."

"Maybe I will." He squeezed her hand. "What's it gonna hurt? Right?"

"Right." She grinned up at him. "The worst thing they can say is no."

Maybe that was it though; maybe he didn't want the rejection. Rejection had been such a big part of his life. "You're right. I gotta get over the fear of people thinking my ideas are shit."

"It happens to everybody, J. Doesn't mean anyone is saying they don't want you in their lives. They're just saying that maybe that's not for them at that moment. Positive thinking." She leaned up and kissed him on the cheek.

"Get outta here with that shit," he teased as he

curled his arm around her neck and pulled her close. "I don't know about you, but I have a sweet tooth."

"I got all the sweet you need, right here," she teased back, winding her arms around his neck and pulling him down for a kiss.

"THIS IS THE kind of sweet tooth I was talking about." He moaned as he took a bite of his banana split.

"This is amazing." She answered his moan with one of her own as she took a bite of her brownie à la mode.

They were quiet as they both tore into their ice cream. As Jared slowed down, he began speaking. "How's the demo business going for you?"

That was the last question she'd expected from him. She didn't talk about this with many people, and as far as she could recall, the two of them had never had a conversation about it. "I love it," she answered honestly. "I love to sing, it's one of my passions, but I don't want anything else that goes with it. I don't want people telling me what size to be, what food to eat, what color my hair should be, and I sure as fuck don't want fans trying to control my life. This lets me do something I love while having none of the commitment." She winked. "And if there's a great song I think Hannah might like, I tell her."

"You little spy."

"You have to do what you have to do in this business," she argued.

"I think the country business is way more cutthroat than the rock business, to be honest." He took another bite of his ice cream. "There seems to be a lot of back-door deals."

"You have no fucking idea. I'm glad Hannah's taken this time off. She needed it to regroup, and to be honest, so did I. It's difficult advocating for her all the time when all I want to do is tell people to shove it up their ass."

"I think that's what I love about you more than anything else, you're a bulldog. You protect Hannah with everything you have, and you make no excuses for it. At the same time, you keep her honest about her own shit."

She dropped her spoon. "If you haven't noticed, Jared, I do the same shit for you."

He hadn't noticed, and he felt stupid for not noticing, but now that she'd said it, he realized she spoke the truth. His life had completely changed when he'd met her, and it'd changed for the better. "You have no idea how much I appreciate that." He leaned over, kissing her, tasting the chocolate against her lips.

Shell breathed easier than she had in a long time. For the first time in months, there wasn't a voice in the back of her head telling her not to completely let her guard down because he'd hurt her before. There wasn't that feeling that this could all be ripped from her. Instead, she felt hope and like this would work out. It was the best feeling she'd ever had in her life.

They finished up their ice cream and took off down the street, walking back towards his truck. "It's starting to get dark. I guess I should take you home," he said as they made their way back into the parking garage.

He leaned up against the quarter-panel, pulling her

between his thighs and giving her another kiss as he ran his hands down her back.

She leaned up so that she spoke in his ear. "What if I told you I don't want to go home tonight? What if I told you instead that I want to go home with you?"

"I'd say that sounds like the best news I've heard all day."

She kissed his neck. "Then please, take me home."

# Chapter Twenty-Seven

O N THE WAY to his condo, it had gotten darker, and clouds had rolled in, signaling a spring storm. They could feel the electricity of it cackling, almost like the electricity between the two of them.

Jared led her up the condo, never letting go of her hand. When they walked inside, he finally dropped it to take his jacket off and throw his keys on the counter. "I didn't even give you the tour last time you were here," he told her, putting his hands in his back pocket, trying to keep them to himself.

"I only need to know where the bedroom is." Her eyes were bright, her cheeks were flushed, and he wanted to make sure that look stayed on her face.

He didn't know what he had done to deserve this, didn't know what he'd done to deserve her, but he wasn't going to be a dumbass again. There were only so many chances she would give him, so many times he could expect her to look the other way. "C'mere," he whispered, crooking his finger at her.

She came to him, not asking any questions.

The trust she gave him never failed to bring him to his knees. Picking her up, he placed her on one of the high-top chairs that he used at the breakfast bar. Using his hands, he tilted her chin up to him and melded their lips together, coaxing hers apart, allowing him to slide his tongue into her mouth, allowing him to move her head to his liking. Slowly, his hands moved from her chin, down her shoulders, her sides, her stomach, to the edge of her T-shirt. Once there, he fisted the shirt in his hands and pulled his lips away from hers, lifting the material off her body, leaving her in a black lace bra.

"Damn, I like that." He caressed her flesh through the lace, watching as her nipple hardened against his palm, liking the way it poked out between the scraps of lace. "Feel good?" he asked, taking in the look on her face.

"Yeah." She nodded, putting her hands behind her on the flat countertop, using it prop herself up and thrust her chest towards him.

Jared took the hint and unhooked the front clasp of the bra, sliding the straps down so that it hung at her wrists. "Don't move your hands; keep offering those tits up to me."

She did as he asked, not moving a muscle.

Taking his bottom lip in between his teeth, he widened his stance and leaned forward, curling his fingers around hers on the countertop. As he leaned forward, it put him at eye level with her chest. He quirked a brow and swooped in, grasping the hard flesh between his teeth, using his tongue to stroke against the nub before letting go with his teeth and sucking deeply.

Her head lolled back on her neck, and it felt like he spent hours there, caressing, biting, licking, and sucking. She felt boneless, more turned on than she'd ever felt in her life.

"Jared," she breathed loudly, trying to move her hands so that she could push herself further into his mouth.

He refused to release her hands and bit down harder when her legs came off of the seat and curled around his waist, bringing her hot heat in touch with his hard body.

"Goddamn, Shell," he cursed as he pulled away from her. His hands went to her thighs and he lifted her up around his waist as he walked towards the bedroom.

SHELL HAD NEVER been so excited in her life as she was when he set her down on the soft cushion of what she assumed was his bed. No light was on in the room, and because it was cloudy outside and rain beat against the window, it gave them a soft, muted glow. It was enough to make her think she was in the middle of her own romance novel.

Watching as Jared straightened and rid himself of not only his shirt, but his jeans and boots, she went to work on hers. If he got naked, she damn well wanted to get naked too. Within minutes both of them were as bare as the day they were born, and he'd scooted her further back on the bed before taking a knee and sinking against her.

"You're so beautiful," he praised her, his stubbled cheek rubbing against her shoulder as he buried his mouth in her neck.

She flexed her fingers against his shoulders as he nipped at her sensitive flesh, soothing the burn with the soft lash of his tongue. It was a mysterious mix of hard and soft, and she didn't know which one she would get. Keeping her on edge and guessing seemed to be his game today. When his mouth moved down her chest, again capturing her turgid flesh, her hand did some exploring of its own and circled around his hard length. She moaned as it jumped in her hand, and so did he.

"Damn, that feels good," he mumbled against her skin. "Don't stop."

She began moving her hand up and down his length, using the lubrication that was already there to ease her strokes. When his breathing picked up and it became a sharp inhale through his nose, she used her palm, sliding it over the tip before going back down against his hard flesh. Squirming against him, she tried to get closer, wanting to be as close to him as she'd ever been.

He trailed one hand down her stomach, and using two fingers, he breached her body, groaning against her flesh. "Fuck, Shell, you're so wet."

"I know." She scissored her legs against him. "I want you. Please don't make me wait!"

They were the most honest words she'd ever spoken. She did want him—in every way that she could have him. That scared her more than she cared to admit, but she'd never lived her life playing it safe.

He withdrew his fingers from her body and lifted

himself up on one arm. Pushing her hand from his dick, he used the hand he'd had inside her body to give himself a few strokes before he leveled himself on the bed and pressed home.

It had never been like this with another woman, not in all the years he'd been having sex or been in relationships, it had *never* been like this with anyone else. He pumped his hips, pulling in, pushing out, as he cupped her face in his hand, bringing their lips together. His other hand grasped her fingers, pushing them deeper into the mattress as he owned her body.

"Deeper," she begged. "Faster."

Digging her heels into his lower back, she urged him on.

He let go of her hand and pulled the lower part of his body up, resting on his knees and thighs, leaning so that he could grasp the headboard. Using it for leverage, he thrust deeply into her, causing them both to groan.

"Stop holding back." She moved her hands up her own body, grasping the tips of her breasts, twisting them with her own hands.

He growled as he watched, his measured strokes becoming haphazard and faster. His rhythm faltered when she gasped loudly and squeezed his body with hers. A loud yell from him, and he was spilling himself deeply into her body.

As they lay there, both trying to catch her breath, she told him what was in her heart. "I love you."

But there was a part of her that wondered when they'd actually get to the root of the matter, when they'd actually have it out.

# Chapter Twenty-Eight

"SORRY I'M LATE," she whispered as she had a seat next to Jared in his Monday meeting. "The demo session ran a few minutes over, and then I hauled ass over here."

"It's good. I know this one is really out of your way, and I appreciate that you come to it." He put his arm around her neck, pulling her close to him.

Since the other night at his condo, they'd been spending more time together. In one way, it felt like they were closer than they had been, but in a completely other way, she felt as if there was this rift between them. She hadn't been able to put her finger on it, and she hadn't wanted to bring it up with him, because she knew when he asked her what was wrong, she wouldn't be able to explain herself. Snapping herself out of it, she gave her full attention to the meeting, because she learned a lot at these things too.

"Today, we have someone who came to me and told me they wanted to speak," the leader said as he nodded towards a woman Shell recognized as one of the wives.

She'd seen her at other meetings and had noticed she was always with her husband. He was with her today, and he grasped her hand, nodding towards her. It was powerful, the way they gave each other the strength to do what needed to be done. She watched as the woman took a deep breath and squared her shoulders.

"I normally stay quiet at these things, because honestly, I feel often that this isn't necessarily my fight. I feel like I'm just a passenger on this ride, but over the weekend, my mother-in-law came to visit, and she said some things that upset me. She told me that I enable him, that I'm his problem." Tears were apparent in the woman's eyes. "And I just need to know that there's another spouse here, woman or man, who knows where I'm coming from. I love this man, he's my life, and I've dedicated so much of my time to try and help him. I struggle with depression now because of the things this disease has put us through, and to hear her say that…" The woman stopped speaking, the tears taking over as she shook her head.

Shell watched as the other woman's shoulders shook—giving in to the emotions she was feeling. Shell also listened as not one other person opened their mouth, not one person offered to tell this woman that they got where she was coming from, when she knew that over half the people in the room did. She figured that was because so often, as someone who loved an addict, you had to keep your mouth shut, bite your tongue, and learn to live with it. That's what so many people told them. Not wanting this woman to feel like she was alone—and knowing that she wasn't—Shell did something she'd never done in one of these meetings. She spoke up.

"No, I get it," Shell said quietly from where she sat next to Jared, smiling softly at the other woman, offering comradery where many times there wasn't any.

He turned, giving her his full attention. She'd never spoken in these meetings—ever, and he wanted to know what she thought more than he wanted to breathe his last breath. Maybe here, in this moment, he could see what the disconnect was between them, because since their last encounter, he'd been feeling it too.

Shell looked at the woman head-on, not glancing over at Jared. "You love this man who is everything to you, and then you realize you're second best, you're never gonna be as important as the drugs he takes." She stopped for a moment and licked her lips, gathering her thoughts before she continued. "Then you ask yourself, what's my damage? Why do I keep doing this to myself? Why do I keep letting him and the drug dictate my life? When did I become not good enough? When did his love of that trump his love of me? How do you believe that again? How do you believe they can ever love something as much as they love the feeling that drug gives them?"

Jared felt like he'd been kicked in the stomach as he heard her continue speaking.

"Or better yet, was I *ever* good enough? Then you come to places like this, and you learn you're an enabler. Fuck if that doesn't suck too. Because then it becomes your fault. It's easy for people to lay blame at your feet. They ask, why don't you love him enough? Why don't you make things easier? Why do you let him do this to himself?"

Tears were falling now, and her voice was hoarse as she kept going.

"But the question I ask myself is why doesn't *he* love *me* enough? What does that drug have that I don't have? What makes me be second best when I've given everything to this person who walks all over me and then pretty much laughs behind my back, and I cry wondering if they're going to live or not?"

She swallowed roughly, wiping some of the tears away.

"Don't get me wrong, I know I'm not a victim here, but this kills me. How can this man who I love more than life, who I've given everything to—my love, my body, my trust, my soul, fuck, *myself* to—not care. How can he not look back and see I was there with him as he lay in a shower puking up drugs so that he wouldn't die." She finally looked at him, and the pain in her eyes was enough to bring him to his knees.

"Because I think that what a lot of you are missing here, who don't get it, is that once you die, you're gone. You don't come back. The ones who love you are left holding nothing. They're left with memories and night-mares and questions of why and what they could have done to change things. When really it's your own fucking selfishness that we're dealing with. You're gone, it doesn't matter to you, and we're left dealing with the feelings and holding ourselves together without the people we love. How fucking fair is that? How can you keep telling us that you love us when you refuse to make a change that would do nothing but benefit us?"

She looked around at every addict and every partner. "People call you brave for making a change in your lives, and I applaud that because I know it's hard." She glanced at Jared. "But it would be nice if y'all could step out of your self-imposed *why me* cave and realize that loving you, the addict, is even harder. In the end, sometimes we're left with nothing but a casket, a box of pictures, and memories that will fade over time. You think you get it? You have no fucking idea."

She got up and made her way to the exit, leaving Jared floored as he tried to come to grips with what she'd said.

# Chapter Twenty-Nine

L EAVING NASHVILLE WHILE he and Shell weren't on great terms fucking sucked. After she'd left the meeting, he'd tried to confront her, tried to get her to tell him what was going through her mind, but she'd been too raw. Hell, he'd been raw too, trying to figure out how she'd kept all of this hidden, and how she'd kept her feelings to herself while still giving him pieces of her.

"You look rough," Garrett told him, having a seat next to him in the van that was taking them from the airport to the record company.

"Shell and I had a bit of an argument the other night, and I didn't even know we were having it." And that was true. Maybe he'd been stupid for believing things were fine, that even though they hadn't hashed out the biggest differences, they were strong.

"I hate when that shit happens. Wanna talk about it?" Normally, Garrett wasn't the kind of man to want to be feely with anyone but his wife; however, he would make an exception for Jared.

Jared sighed, folding his arms over his chest. It had

always been, and still was, a defense mechanism. "She came with me to a meeting, and while we were there, a wife started talking. I don't know what happened, but all of a sudden, Shell started talking, and all this stuff that I'm assuming she's kept inside started pouring out. After she was done, she left, and she hasn't talked to me since."

"Damn, man, how long ago was that?"

Jared picked at his jeans. "Two days ago." He swallowed roughly. "I know I've not done a lot of things right with her, but I thought we were in a good place, and I thought we were moving ahead and moving past all the shit." He sighed. "I don't know what to do at this point. Then we had to leave this morning." He leaned forward and put his head in his hands, his voice rough. "I don't know what to do, and I fucking refuse to lose her. We've worked so hard to make shit work."

Garrett searched for the right words to offer his friend, but there weren't any. "I wish I could tell you that things are going to be okay and that things will work themselves out, but I don't know what to say."

"I don't know either. I don't know where we go from here because she won't talk to me." He growled in frustration. "This is what she does, and in the past I've let her do it, but fuck, I need her to be all in with me right now."

"I'm telling you, I've seen you two together recently. She *is* all in with you. I think she got scared." Garrett tried to think back to the things he'd heard Shell and Hannah talking about. "Do you think it was getting too serious for her?"

"Fuck, man, it's serious for me. I got her ass a ring," he admitted lowly.

Garrett's mouth opened in shock, and he pulled his sunglasses down. "What?"

"I got her a ring at Valentine's Day." He chuckled in a self-deprecating way. "I've been carrying this fucking thing around with me in my pocket for months, and I thought we were finally at a point where she might accept it, and now this bullshit."

Garrett could tell Jared was getting irritated and his anger was getting the better of him. He wanted to calm him down, because when Jared got irritated on the West Coast, it was dangerous.

"Give her and yourself some time," he told him. "You love her, she loves you, every once in a while you're gonna fight. You think Hannah and I don't?"

Jared faced him, his eyes flashing. "No, I do know that you fight, but she doesn't ignore you like a brat."

"Oh Jesus, Jared. She does; she stomps her feet and screams too. This isn't out of the ordinary behavior. She'll get over it, you'll get over, and then you'll fuck each other's brains out and be done."

Jared shook his head, because he wasn't completely sure.

FLYING INTO CALIFORNIA for the day was always a pain in the ass, because it meant they had meetings. Neither he nor Garrett felt that their home was in California anymore, and he was seriously considering selling his house.

Jared flopped on his couch, listening to the silence. This was the time when he needed to work his program. He felt the walls closing in, and he wondered what he would do with himself. Everything in him wanted to call Shell; he wanted to hear her voice, see her face, anything. He opened his phone and ran his thumb along his contacts until he saw her name, and dialed. Like he knew it would, it went straight to voicemail. He cleared his throat and started to speak.

"I'm not going to pretend I understand what the fuck I put you through, and I'm not going to pretend you walking of there didn't hurt me, but what I want more than anything is for you to pick up the damn phone. Pick up the phone and call me. I want to work this shit out. I need to work this shit out," he begged. "I love you."

Disengaging the call, he threw his head back against the cushion of the couch. Tomorrow, he could go home. He just had to make it through tonight. His phone vibrated in his hand, and immediately, he hoped it was Shell. Glancing down, he saw it was Garrett, and a text came through.

*EJ has RSV and they are putting him in the hospital. I'm heading back to Nashville tonight. See you in day or so.*

Jared's stomach dropped. Hopefully that was why Shell hadn't answered his call, because she was dealing with drama at home. Then he thought about EJ—the little nephew he never knew he wanted—in the hospital, and he wondered why things always had to be so crazy for them.

*If you need anything let me know. I'm here for you, in whatever capacity you need.*

Just like that, the walls were closing in again. He needed to get out of his house and find a place, as far away from town as he could to run. He needed to get his blood pumping and feel it flowing through his veins. He needed to clear his head, because right now, he could taste the drugs he would love to take. It would be so easy to call a friend and ask them to bring something over; it would be so easy to let himself play the victim again.

Getting up from the couch, he changed into shorts, a T-shirt, and his running shoes. Opening the door, he came face-to-face with someone who had their hand up, knuckles read to knock.

"Murph?"

He was shocked the man who had provided him with the heroin that contributed to his OD was here, in the flesh, right now, when he least needed to see him.

"Train, dude, how about you invite an old friend in?"

Jared wished he was strong enough to say no, but he wasn't. He stepped back from the door and made enough room for the other man to come in, hating himself the entire time.

# Chapter Thirty

JARED KNEW HE should make Murph leave. He'd been here all night, and they'd been rehashing the "good times" they'd had. It was hollow for Jared. He didn't remember any of those times as good. This far into his recovery, he could finally admit that the partying hadn't been fun, but it'd been comfortable. That was a hell of a revelation.

Finally Murph got up to leave. "It was good seeing you again, Train." He held out his hand for Jared to give him a shake, and when Jared did, he felt plastic against his palm.

"What's this?" he asked, freezing when he saw a bag of heroin.

"My gift to you. Welcome home, dude." Murph grinned, knowing exactly what he'd done, and grabbed his stuff, leaving Jared alone as he walked out the front door.

*Fuck,* Jared thought to himself. This was his test; this was what he'd been waiting on. He'd known at some point there would be a test. He just hadn't thought it would be at the lowest possible time he'd been at in a while.

Sitting down at his breakfast bar, he put the plastic packet down in front of him on the countertop and stared. What he decided to do here would change his life forever. His mouth watered as he flipped the packet over and over in his hand, running it through his fingers. He knew it was a bad idea, but he opened the packed and dumped it out onto the granite. He licked his lips, almost able to taste it. Reaching into his wallet, he pulled out a credit card and started lining it up, cutting it and sectioning it off. It was so familiar to him. He rolled his head on his neck and looked away from the rows. They were inviting to him, telling him that if he would just roll up a dollar, bend over, and take the hit, things wouldn't bother him anymore. He wouldn't be worried about Shell, EJ, or anything else. His loneliness would be gone, and he would feel good about himself.

The sane, rational part of his mind told him he was fucking dumb. That if he took this hit, he'd be throwing away everything he'd worked so hard for the past few months. He berated himself, wondering why he couldn't commit to being clean, but he sure as fuck could commit to being a fuck-up. His eyes went to his phone, and he picked it up, once again dialing Shell's number.

WALKING OUT OF the hospital, Shell was exhausted. Luckily EJ was going to be released later on in the day, but the night before had been scary. When Garrett had showed up, she'd known she could go home, but she hadn't wanted to go home to an empty house. Stepping into the parking lot, her phone came alive, notifying her of calls and texts, and it started ringing again. When she saw Jared's face, she knew she had to answer.

"Hey," she answered softly, walking quicker to her car. Once she got there, she got inside and shut herself there.

"How are you?" he asked.

She could tell by the way he spoke to her that something was going on. There was a strained tone to his voice she hadn't heard in a long time. Immediately, she was on alert and sitting up straight in her driver's seat. "Jared, talk to me. What's going on?"

"Nothing, feeling sorry for myself. I need to get back to Nashville."

"C'mon, J, FaceTime me," she told him, disconnecting the call. Her fingers shook as she re-dialed. She breathed a sigh of relief when he answered. "What's going on?"

"Murph came by last night."

Her blood ran cold. She knew exactly who Murph was, and she wondered immediately what he'd done. "Did you do anything?" she asked, trying to keep the accusation out of her voice.

He turned the phone so that she could see what was in front of him. "Not yet."

Suddenly she was tired, so fucking tired of this. She couldn't even get angry with him, couldn't even begin to tell him how disappointed she was. What she'd said the other night at the meeting was the truth. "Aren't I good enough not to do that for?"

"You are, but it still tempts me." The honesty was in his voice.

Her tone was resigned. "But is it worth it? Is it really worth it, Jared? Losing me? Losing your friends, your family. Is it worth it? Is that line of heroin or cocaine, whatever the fuck it is—is it worth it? I can't fight for you if you don't want to fight for yourself."

A million things went through his mind. "Why the fuck do I keep doing this?"

"I don't know," she sniffled, letting the tears she'd been trying to hold back fall. "I don't know how I can prove I love you anymore than I already have. The question you have to ask yourself is are *you* worth it? Do you finally feel like *you're* worth it?"

"I want to believe I am."

"Then make your decision, J. This is one I can't make for you, but know that if you make the wrong decision, I'm done. I'm completely and fully done with you. It will be hard, and it will break my heart—but there are no more chances."

She disconnected the call and leaned her head against the steering wheel, letting the tears fall.

SHELL WAS DROWNING in her own misery, telling herself that if Jared wanted to choose drugs over her, there was nothing she could do about it. A knock on her window startled her, and she lifted her head up, seeing Hannah standing there. Rolling down the window, she pulled her bottom lip between her teeth to keep it from trembling.

"Yeah?"

Hannah frowned and looked as if she wanted to say something but didn't. Instead she reached into the SUV, handing Shell an envelope. "You need to read this. It's time."

When she looked at the envelope, she realized it was the one Jared had left for her on Valentine's Day. Hannah gave her a timid smile and turned on her heel, going back into the hospital.

Once again alone, Shell flipped it between her hands, stomach clenching at the thought of reading it. But what else was there to do?

# Chapter Thirty-One

ER HANDS SHOOK as she ripped into the sealed package and pulled the letter out. It wasn't long like she thought it would be, but she recognized the slanted script he wrote in. Wiping underneath her eyes, she sighed and brought the letter up so that she could see the words.

*Shell,*

*I've told you over and over again that I'm not the type of man who reveals his feelings. I was always taught as a kid not to, that it didn't help anything and that no matter what you told people, they still had the ability to break your heart. They had the ability to leave, and then you'd be alone again. So I never told anyone how I felt.*

*Until you.*

*And even now, I can't tell you how I feel in person like I should, but that's something I'm going to work on. That's something I don't ever want you to question, and if you do question it…remind me of this. Remind me of how fucking empty I've felt the last few months. Remind me of how I've cried myself to sleep, wanting you with me. Don't let me fuck things up. This is me begging for help and telling you that I love you more than anything in this world.*

*My world begins and ends with you.*

*Don't give up on me.*

*I love you.*

*Jared*

Breathing deeply, she wasn't sure what she should do. Closing her eyes, she sent up a small prayer, asking whatever spiritual being there was to show her what to do. To show her if it was worth taking one more chance.

Picking up her phone, she texted to him the only thing she could think of.

*I love you, but you have to love yourself enough to walk away from your temptations. I'm reminding you of how lonely you were and how your world begins and ends with me. My world begins and ends with you. Please don't break my heart.*

The tears continued to fall as she made her way out of the parking lot, towards her home. Nothing would get solved until he was home, and it wouldn't do her any good to worry about it.

"I NEED OUT of here today," Jared told the airline attendant. "It's an emergency."

He had to get home to Nashville; he had to get to

Shell. As he'd entered the airport, he'd received her text message and knew she'd finally read his letter. It was the sign he'd been waiting on. He knew right then what he was supposed to do—he had made the right decision to flush the heroin down the toilet. His hands had been clammy and shaky as he had scooped up the white powder and deposited in the toilet. It had taken everything he'd had in him not to lick his hands and try, just once more, to feel the euphoric feeling. But he couldn't; he was sick of being *that guy*. He was sick of being the fuck-up. For once, he wanted to be who everybody thought he was. He wanted to be someone everyone else could be proud of. He would pass this test, he would go to Nashville and he would have the life he was meant to have.

"Okay, we can get you on one leaving in thirty minutes, but you're going to have to run for it," the attendant told him.

"Whatever you got, I'll make it."

His heart pounded in his chest as he ran full-speed through the terminal, making his way through the gate right before it closed. No matter how fast this plane flew, it couldn't get him back to Nashville fast enough.

SHELL HADN'T HEARD a word from Jared since she'd texted him, and to say she was nervous was an understatement. There were a million scenarios running through her head, and she just wanted to hear his voice, to know that he was good, that he was okay, but she was standing strong about taking the step. Flipping her phone over and over on her thigh, she'd made the decision to call Hannah when her doorbell rang. Getting up, she threw open the door.

There, almost exactly like he'd been on Valentine's Day, Jared stood there, holding flowers out to her. This time he wasn't wearing a suit, but there was a huge smile on his face.

"I'm here. I choose you, I choose clean, I choose to be the person so many people never thought I could or would be," he said in a quick rush of words.

Tears came again for her, this time happy ones, as she threw herself into his arms, wrapping herself around him. "I've never been so happy to see you," she choked out, her mouth buried in his neck.

"I've never been so happy to see you either," he answered as he pushed them back into the living room and shut the door. He disentangled their arms from each other and guided them over to the couch. Putting he flowers on the coffee table, he grabbed her hands, looking at her.

"I've been going crazy trying to figure out your decision and what you were going to do," she cried, using their hands to wipe away some of the many tears she had shed in the past few days.

"I wanted to make sure it was my decision," he explained. "I wanted to make sure it was mine and mine alone. At some point, I have to stand on my own two feet, and I have to make sure I can trust myself. I did it, I made the right decision."

"You did, babe." She let his hands go and cupped his cheeks in the palm of her hands, kissing him softly. "You did it."

"I did," He smiled, this one reaching his eyes. "I did," he repeated. "But I wonder if I hurt you into coming into my own. I'm scared because you ran from that meeting when things got serious."

"I did run," she admitted. "And I'm not proud of it, but I had to get those feelings out, I had to tell you those words. There was a part of me that was holding back from you, not giving you everything I could. I can do that now. I feel like I'm important to your life," she sobbed. "I feel like I matter more than the drugs— finally," she choked out a laugh.

"Oh babe, you've always meant more to me than the drugs. I just had to find the strength to let myself feel."

"Do you feel it?" She put her hand up to his heart. "Do you feel how much I love you?"

He nodded. "And I feel how much I love you."

She threw herself at him again. "Please don't do this to me again," she begged.

"I can't make promises I might not be able to keep, because I know myself, but I can promise you that you'll never have to wonder how much I love you again. You'll never wonder how important you are to me."

She could live with that, and they could move forward as a couple with that.

# Chapter Thirty-Two

S HE SLOWLY LIFTED her arms up to him. "I don't want to hold back from you anymore. I want us to be exactly who we are with one another."

"I want that too, more than you know." He circled her arms around his neck and pushed her up against the back of the couch in her living room.

For a moment he looked at her, almost as if he were memorizing every part of her face, every hair on her head, and each fleck of color that showed in her eyes. When he was done, he leaned forward, capturing her lips with his.

Shell sighed. This wasn't the fast and out-of-control feeling they'd had for the past few months. The way he worked her mouth was slow and deliberate. She could feel the emotion he was trying to convey to her, she could feel the reverent way he ran his hands down her body and picked her up so that she sat on the back of the couch. She struggled for a moment to keep her balance, but trusted him to hold her up.

"I've got you," he whispered against her lips, his

arms tightening around her. "I'm not gonna let you fall."

And she knew instinctively that she could trust him. His arms and hands were strong against her back as she leaned against them, letting her fingers play in the hair at the nape of his neck. "Take your shirt off," she told him.

He quirked a brow. It wasn't often that Shell told him what to do when they were intimate, and the order intrigued him. He let go of her and slipped his shirt over his head, grunting as she hopped down, turned them around, and leaned his body against the couch.

"Let me do this for you, let me show you how much I want you." She dropped to her knees in front of him.

"Fuck," he ground out, and she hadn't even done anything yet.

The side of her mouth titled as her fingers went to the buckle of the belt he wore. She took her time unbuckling it before unbuttoning and pushing his clothes down his thighs. She stared at his hard length until he pushed against the back of her head.

"It ain't gonna do any tricks until you put your mouth on it, sweetheart."

She shook her head, a smile on her face as she grasped the base, holding it straight out, and moved her hand up and down for two strokes.

JARED'S KNEES WEAKENED, and he gave his full weight to the couch, throwing his head back as he finally felt her warm mouth encompass most of his cock. He grasped the back of her head, twining his fingers in her hair, pulling her closer to him as he pumped his hips.

"God, Shell," he moaned. Sex was amazing, but sometimes head was even more amazing, and Shell didn't do it a lot, so he knew that when she did, he was in for a treat. She made a tight circle with her lips and sucked harshly against him. The feeling almost made him jump out of skin.

"That's it," he encouraged as he pried his eyes open and glanced down at her. "Suck it hard."

Abandoning her hair, he took one hand and moved it down her body, cupping her breast in his palm, running his thumb over the puckered nipple he could feel. "You like this?" he asked.

She nodded against his length, breathing through her nose, allowing her throat to relax as she took him in deeper.

"I like this too." He groaned when she let her tongue bathe him, running up and down the underside.

Finally, not able to breathe anymore, she released him and used her hand to jack up and down.

"Tell me," he commanded, his fingers roughly pulling against the fabric of her shirt.

"So hot," she moaned, throwing her head back as he moved his hands down to the hem and pulled her shirt off her body. "Doing this to you gets me hot," she admitted as he took his hand and jacked his own cock for several strokes.

"Are you wet?" He grabbed the back of her head and made her face him, forced her to look up into his eyes.

"Very," she moaned as he leaned down and kissed

her on the lips.

As much as he loved her lips wrapped around him, he loved her warm heat just as much. He grabbed her up by the arms and moved them around to the other side of the couch. "Take it off." He indicated everything else she had on.

He did the same as he watched her get naked for him. Once she was naked, he pushed her down onto the cushions and situated her over the arm, on her knees. "You ready, baby?" he asked as he teased her with the head of his length.

She glanced over her shoulder. "Always for you."

Shoving himself home, he knew this was exactly where he needed to be, and he knew without a doubt this was home and would always be home.

# Chapter Thirty-Three

"**Y**OU READY?" JARED asked as he grabbed his jacket and glanced over at Shell. They were on their way to a meeting. One of the two they tried to attend together every week. In the month since they'd finally talked things out, the relationship had been going very well for them. They weren't perfect. He still had times where he wanted her trust and didn't always get it, and she had times where she wanted him to be more emotionally available and she didn't always get it either, but they were working on it.

She grabbed her coffee and bag. They were taking the SUV tonight. "Yup, whenever you are. Don't forget that afterwards we need to run by Garrett and Hannah's so I can give EJ that stuffed red panda I picked up for him at the Nashville Zoo."

That was another change in their relationship. They were finding things they liked to do together besides spending time in bed. A switch had been flipped, and they were becoming the couple he'd always wanted to be. When he looked at Garrett's parents and Garrett and

Hannah, they were partners, and for the first time he felt like he and Shell were becoming that. He didn't hide things from her to make it easier, and she didn't hide things from him not to hurt his feelings.

"We'll go," he laughed, leaning in to kiss her on the cheek. "And you can give it to him this time. I know I swooped in and gave him that Dragon and became his favorite for a week."

She wrinkled her nose and harrumphed. "I bought that for him. I'm still pissed at you for that."

He put his arm around her shoulders and brought her in for a kiss. "You forgave me for that, or don't you remember?"

She did remember. He'd done naughty things to her that night. Her eyes were bright as she smiled up at him. What they had was good, and she tried not to wait on the other shoe to drop. "Let's go." She grabbed his hand, pulling him out of the condo.

They got into his SUV and made their way across town for the meeting they were going to. Once they got there and parked, they walked inside, both waving to people they had become friendly with in the past few weeks. It amazed him how welcoming everyone had been to Shell, how girlfriends and wives had sought her out and given her tips, told her not to give up on him. They'd talked through each time one of those women had come to her and told her what to expect from him. He appreciated it more than he could say. He found them a seat, and they got comfortable, waiting on the meeting to start.

"ONE OF THE things we're going to talk about tonight is expectation," Trey, the leader, said after the preliminaries were said and done.

Jared liked this particular meeting more so than some of the others. This one was always like a huge group therapy session. All of them had issues they needed to talk about, and each week the group had a theme.

"Does anyone know what I mean by that?"

There was something that had been bothering him for a while, and Jared felt like this was the time for him to speak up, that this was a safe environment for him to do so. If he and Shell could talk anywhere and get the support they needed, it was here.

"I feel like there's an expectation for me to fail," he said quietly.

"Okay." Trey faced him and Shell, looking at the two of them. "Can you expand on that? If you're feeling that way, then someone else in here is too. Let's talk about it."

"This woman," he grabbed Shell's hand and held it tightly, "has been with me through a lot of shit. I've put her through the ringer. I don't want you to think I'm asking for blind forgiveness, because I'm not, but I feel like she and most of my friends have this expectation that I'm going to fail. They are supportive, way more supportive than I probably would be if I had someone like me in my own life, but I can see it in the way she looks at me sometimes. I can tell by the way she makes plans but doesn't make them too far out." He glanced over at her. "Babe, I'm not asking for unbridled trust, because I know that's a lot and I've been a fuck-up for more years than I've been good, but I want you to feel like we can make plans. When you hold back from me, you hold back from us, and I think we've had enough holding us back to last a lifetime."

"What do you have to say to that?" Trey asked as he scooted his chair closer to them, to give them one-on-one time.

Shell wasn't sure what to say, so she took a moment to get her thoughts together. "I will admit I'm scared to make plans with him. At one point, in my mind, I had the wedding dress picked out, kids' names, and where we would be living, but then it all came crashing down around me. There's still a part of me, on difficult nights, that can close my eyes and still see him in that shower fighting for his life as we waited for the paramedics to get there." She stopped and looked at Jared. "My unwillingness to make plans with you hasn't been an effort to hurt you, it's been an effort to protect myself."

"I know." Jared tightened his grip on her. "And I'm not asking for us to make plans for a year down the road, or even six months, but I want you to know that you can count on me. If you don't give me a little bit, it hinders me instead of helping me. You don't bring a bag to stay at my condo; I don't have a key to your house. Those are things I want; they are small tokens of your belief that I can do this."

She felt as if she'd been smacked in the face. Until he'd pointed this out, she hadn't realized how tightly she was holding herself from him, even though she gave him the words and actions of love every day. There was still a part of her she held so tight that if she didn't let it go, he'd never be able to invade it. "You don't have a key to my house?" The fact that she hadn't given him one spoke volumes. She didn't even realize that until he'd mentioned it.

He smiled patiently, more patiently than she would have. "No, and I haven't pressured you for it because I know I did things I shouldn't have done, I know I took your trust and threw it down the toilet. I let stupid things affect me. I've made a conscious decision not to even let those things enter my thoughts anymore. My parents don't want me, that's fine, but you do, and I want you too. I'm putting everything I have into this, Shell. Give me a little bit back."

"I'm sorry; I didn't realize I was doing it in such a way that was all or nothing. I promise you, I'll work on it, and as soon as we leave here, we'll go get you a key made."

Trey clapped both of them on the back. "Communication is the key to all of this, and as long as you both keep communicating with one another, you're going to make it."

She leaned over to Jared as Trey made his way over to another couple. "I feel like we are," she whispered.

He flashed her the smile she knew was just for her. "I think we are too."

# Chapter Thirty-Four

THAT NIGHT, THEY lay in bed in his condo while she was doing work on Harmony's social media and he was going over guitar mockups. Recently he'd signed a contract with a guitar company to release custom versions of the guitars he liked to play.

"EJ's face when I handed him that red panda was the best thing ever." She laughed, remembering their afternoon.

"I know." He cracked up. "And when Garrett went to grab it from him so that we could eat dinner, I almost think that was Reaper looking back at Reaper. Scary to think what that little dude might be like in a few years. I know how Garrett was, and if his son is anything like him, those two have their hands full."

She closed her laptop, leaning back against the pillow. "I'm so sick of working tonight; actually I'm sick of everything." She laughed. "I don't want any responsibility for like, three days."

He grinned over at her before he reached into the drawer of his bedside table. "It's ironic that you say that to me. Someone I know has a birthday next weekend."

"Who's that?" she played along. "Surely to God it's not someone turning twenty-seven. Right?"

"I wouldn't have thought she was a day over twenty-one, the way her tits are still perky and the way her ass bounces when she walks."

She threw back her head, laughing loudly. "Oh my God, you're so good for my ego. Whatcha got?" She spied an envelope in his hand.

"Your birthday gift, ya know…if you want it."

She almost tackled him, going up onto her knees and getting over to his side of the bed. "Gimme!"

He held it out of her reach. "Now if this is something you don't want, we can do something else; I just wanted to surprise you. But I want you to know it won't hurt my feelings if you don't want to do this."

"C'mon, J! Let me see what it is."

He handed her the envelope and waited while she opened it.

"*Oh my God!!! Is this for real?*" She screeched at an ear-piercing level.

Jared had never felt so powerful. The excitement made him feel like he was ten feet tall and could lift a thousand pounds. "If you want to, it is."

"Aruba?" she questioned, a huge smile on her face, her eyes wide.

"Yeah, we leave day after tomorrow. I cleared your schedule with Hannah."

Tears pooled in her eyes. "I can't believe you would do this for me. I didn't think you ever paid attention to my mindless complaining."

He grabbed her hands, bringing her down so that their lips were within kissing distance. Digging his fingers into the hair at the nape of her neck, he brought their lips together. "I hear everything you say, baby, and I'm listening. For once, I'm fucking listening."

"You have no idea how much that means to me," she choked out, hugging him tightly to her.

"I know exactly how much it means, because you're listening to me too, and it's a great feeling. I want us to go, have fun, and forget all the bullshit we've had going on the past few months. We both need this."

He was right; they had been through a lot. Personally and professionally, and they did need a break.

"I have to pack!" She hopped up from the bed. "You have to take me home so I can pack." She did her version of a victory dance on the plush carpet in his bedroom.

He laughed loudly as he watched her, enjoying the happiness and excitement on her face. He would have paid a million dollars to have seen this. "We'll set the alarm and head to your house early in the morning. I'll pack here before we go, and then we can leave from your house for the airport the next day. How's that sound?"

She pouted, sitting back down on the bed. "You know I'm not getting any sleep the next two nights? Right? I can't remember ever being this excited in my life!"

Pulling her so that she straddled his waist, he pushed his hips up into her. "If you aren't tired, then I think I know something else we could do to pass the time."

She bit her lip and leaned down so that she could run her hands up his stomach and chest. "I think I like the way you think, Mr. Winston."

He pushed the tank top she wore up and over her head. "Calling me Sir will be just fine."

She squealed as he flipped them over, dragging her panties down her legs. Her fingers went to the waistband of his boxers and pushed them down far enough too, sighing when he entered her. The first thrust was always her favorite part.

"Yes, Sir," she breathed deeply, holding on as he took them on a very familiar ride.

# Chapter Thirty-Five

"THIS PLACE IS paradise." Shell sighed as she kicked her feet in the private pool they had been provided as part of their package deal. She held a fruity drink in one hand and a piece of chocolate in the other.

Jared glanced at her from behind his sunglasses. They had been in Aruba for three days, and her skin had already taken on a golden tone. It made her blonde hair shine brightly and her eyes pop. They'd spent their days being lazy on the beach, snorkeling when they felt like it, walking when they felt like it, or just hanging at the pool as they were doing today. Their nights were hot; most of them, they ended up falling asleep with him buried deeply inside her, both trying to catch their breath. This was the best vacation he'd ever had in his life.

"Yup, I would have to say I agree."

"Are we doing anything today?" she asked as she rolled her head on the lounger so that she looked in his general direction.

"We have dinner tonight on the beach, as long as it

doesn't rain or anything," he told her, pleased that he had one more surprise for her. He'd worked hard on this one.

"Dinner on the beach? What? You never told me we were going to do that. Seriously, J, you're spoiling the shit outta me. When we get back to Nashville, how am I going to acclimate back to regular life?"

"The same way I will." He pulled a face. "Changing EJ's dirty diapers and wondering where the fuck the record company came up with whatever harebrained scheme they present us with."

"Oh yeah." She took a drink. "There it is—the sound of reality crashing down. How about we keep this going for a few more hours?"

That was his plan. They had to head back to Nashville in the morning. She had meetings with Hannah, and the guys had meetings with some local producers who were interested in working on the next Black Friday album. He had to get back to working his program, and hopefully, he and Shell would have something of their own to plan.

GETTING DRESSED FOR dinner that night was one of the most nervous experiences of his life. He wanted to look nice, but he didn't want to look too nice. He didn't want to give anything away, wanted her to be surprised when he went down on one knee and asked her to be his wife.

"Do I look okay?" she asked as she came out of the bathroom.

He turned around so that he could see, and his breath caught in his throat. She wore a blue dress that showed off her tan, her blonde hair, and the light color of her eyes. She'd done some sort of curly do with her hair, and he wanted desperately to make a mess of it later. He hoped like hell he would be able to make a mess of it later.

"You're beautiful, as always."

"And you're hot." She got a good look at him. Khakis and a white button-down shirt, sleeves rolled up to show off the tattoos he had on his arms. "Do we really have to go to dinner?"

"Yes," he answered. He'd paid a ton for this, but at the same time he wanted this to be something she remembered for the rest of her life, not something he sprung on her in bed. This was special. "I want to do this."

"If you're sure."

"I am." He grabbed her hand. "I heard that this place is particularly gorgeous, and this is a once-in-a-lifetime thing. We've gotta do it."

She knew he spoke the truth and followed him along the pathway that took them to the beach. Instead of walking towards the part of the beach where they had been going for days, he directed them up a few stairs and along another pathway. They continued up a few more sets of stairs, and as they crested a hill, Shell gasped. "Holy shit, this view."

"Right?" Jared felt his chest swell with pride.

From where they sat, they could see into the blue

ocean and had a great view of the resort they were staying at. The table was perfect with a white linen tablecloth, flowers native to the region, and candles that cast a soft glow. As the sun went down, he knew it would be even more romantic.

"Welcome, Mr. Jared and Ms. Shell. We've prepared a feast for you tonight," the waiter said as he welcomed them. "We have shrimp, lobster, different kinds of fish, as well as vegetables and indigenous fruit to the area. For dessert we have your special request of a chocolate mousse cake with strawberries, chocolate sauce, and vanilla ice cream. Please, enjoy."

They had a seat and waited for the waiter to leave before Shell reached across the table and grabbed Jared's hand. "You buttering me up? You know that's my favorite dessert ever."

His answer was purposely flippant. "Hoping to get lucky on my last night here."

"I'm a sure thing. You didn't have to go all out, but I'm glad you did." She took a drink of the fruity concoction she'd been drinking all week. "I sure am gonna miss this stuff."

He had to agree.

"Is it time for dessert?" she asked as they cleared the table off.

"Always here for the sweets, aren't you?"

"I haven't indulged lately, and it sounds divine," she defended herself, looking up as the waiter from earlier brought them a plate to the table.

"Your dessert."

She looked up, thanking him for everything, and they talked for a few seconds before he made a hasty getaway. "Come on," she told Jared. "Grab a spoon and let's demolish this."

Spoon poised, she noticed for the first time that something was written on the plate in the chocolate sauce she loved so much and that a box sat next to the plate.

"Will you marry me?" she read aloud.

Shock registered on her face and in her eyes. She glanced up at him, seeing the love written so plainly on his face.

"Will you?" he asked as he grabbed the ring box and got up from his seat.

He walked over to where she sat, pulling her chair back from the table slightly before he went down on one knee beside her, opening up the ring box. She gasped as she saw the rose gold ring.

"I've wanted to give this to you since Valentine's Day, but I had to make sure we were at a good spot, I had to make sure this was going to last," he explained. "I had to make sure I was ready for it, and that you were ready for me. I think we're there, unless I'm completely wrong."

Her eyes met his, and she thrust her hand out to him. "Yes! Yes we're there!"

He fumbled with the box and finally put the ring on her finger. When he did, she tackled him into the sand, but neither one of them cared as their lips met and fingers dived into hair.

"I love you," he told her, pushing back her hair. "I want to live the rest of my life with you, and whatever difficulties we have, I want to go through them with you. With you is so much better than without you."

"I love you too, and I want to be there, no matter how hard it gets." She gazed at the ring over his shoulder as she stretched her fingers. "It's beautiful."

"It's everything you deserve, and nothing could be more beautiful than you."

# Epilogue

*Three Years Later*

"C'MON, SHELL, YOU can do this," he encouraged her, brushing back the wet hair from her forehead.

"No," she heaved, her voice tired. "I can't." She licked her lips, making a grasp for the cup of ice he held.

Grabbing a piece, he ran it over her dry lips and pushed it into her mouth. "You can. You're the strongest woman I've ever known. Look how you've put up with me and my bullshit. You got this, sweetheart."

"I'm so tired." She lolled her head around on her pillow, trying to focus her bleary eyes.

Hannah appeared at her bedside, grabbing her friend's hand. "C'mon, girl, you got this. I know you got this. Your birth plan says no c-section, remember how we argued over that? It's time for you to quit messing around and get this baby out."

Shell's eyes flashed with anger. "This is hard," she argued. "You had a c-section! You don't understand this pain, this tiredness," she yelled as another contraction hit her. "How dare you judge me?"

"You pissed?" Hannah asked, her mouth tilting up in a grin.

"You bet your ass I am!"

Hannah grabbed her leg and indicated for Jared to grab her other. "Good, now use that and give birth to your daughter."

"Push for me, Shell," the doctor said from where she was, ready to catch the baby, they were that close.

Using every bit of anger that coursed through her body, Shell bore down, pushing with everything she had, taking the last twelve hours of agony and putting it into this crunch she made with her stomach muscles. She wanted badly to see this baby. This was a baby they had prayed for. She'd had trouble, hormone levels were low at times, and some bleeding had kept her on bed rest for two weeks, but they'd made it. She knew she had to see this to the end. She wanted this for her and Jared more than she'd ever wanted anything in her life.

"I see the head, c'mon Shell!"

She could feel the energy in the room, she could feel the love that surrounded her, surrounded Jared and little Montgomery—named for the tour stop she'd been conceived on. It was their own private joke, but they loved the name.

Suddenly, she felt the baby drop and waited anxiously for the screams that would tell her she was okay.

"Is she okay?" she asked, leaning back against her pillow, listening intently, dying a little as she didn't hear anything.

Jared's eyes met hers, his equally as scared, and they heard a hard smack, and then the loud wails of a child.

"Thank God." She heaved a sigh, tears falling from her eyes in way she knew she wouldn't be able to stop for hours. "Let me see her."

They laid the baby on her stomach as they prepared Jared to cut the cord.

"Don't pass out on us, buddy," Garrett teased from where he sat next to the bed, taking pictures as Jared did his daddy duties.

The emotion Jared felt couldn't be put into words as he did as the nurses showed him.

HOURS LATER, THE three of them were alone, and Jared held Montgomery in his arms, cuddling her against him.

"She's gorgeous," Shell said sleepily from her bed.

"She looks just like you. Of course she is." He kissed the top of his daughter's head. It was full of blonde hair.

"No wonder I had heartburn so bad." She nodded towards the headful of hair.

"I love you." He got up and walked over to the bed. "I can't thank you for everything you've given me."

"I love you too." She tried not to get emotional, but her hormones were haywire. She scooted over in the bed to make room for both of them. "You've given me everything too. We've been there for each other, in ways that neither one of us ever planned on."

He pushed his knees up and set Montgomery on them so that her eyes could see both of them and her head was supported. "She's a blank slate, Shell. I don't wanna fuck her up," he whispered.

"You're not going to. You're gonna love this little girl the way you love me. The way your family could never love you. You're gonna show her what an amazing man you are." She reached over and grabbed one of Montgomery's hands. "You're going to be her hero."

"What if I fail?" he asked, the emotion thick in his voice.

"Lots of heroes fail—it's how they handle those failures, how fast they get back up, and how they move forward that matters. There's a thin line between a hero and a villain—it's a choice."

"I'm going to do my best to always make the right one," he vowed.

She leaned her head against his shoulder and absorbed this special moment that was theirs. "I'm going to help you make the right one."

They were quiet for a minute before he spoke again. "Thank you."

"For what?" she asked, her voice sleepy.

"For loving me, even when it was hard to."

## The End

# Connect with Laramie

Website:

www.laramiebriscoe.com

Facebook:

www.facebook.com/AuthorLaramieBriscoe

Twitter:

twitter.com/LaramieBriscoe

Pinterest:

www.pinterest.com/laramiebriscoe/

Instagram:

instagram.com/laramie_briscoe

Substance B:

substance-b.com/LaramieBriscoe.html

Mailing List:

http://eepurl.com/Fi4N9

# Coming January 21st, 2016

## Prologue
## Sketch

**"I** LOVE YOU, but I'm no longer *in love* with you, Devin."

The words echo off the hardwood floor I had paid to have put in our home, they bounce off the walls Nina and I had painstakingly painted yellow. I remember the argument we got into about the trim color; an argument I won by tackling her to the, then carpeted, floor and fucking her into submission. What had happened to that couple? When had that changed?

"I don't even know what to say." And I didn't. Shock and something akin to anger boil in my gut. I want to scream and punch, ask what the fuck is wrong with her, but those words won't come. I can't push them past my lips.

She sighs. "That's precisely the problem, Devin; you never know what to say. You never know when you're going to be home, you never know what your schedule is going to be. I can't do this. When was the last time we had sex? When was the last time you told me that you love me? Devin, I'm done."

There it is again. My real name. For the past seven years I've been Sketch. Through my apprenticeship and now at my own shop. Most people don't even know my real fuckin' name, and here she's used it twice in one conversation.

"You're done?" I sound like a parrot, but I can't help it. This shit is coming out of left field for me. I'm standing here like a chump, holding a bouquet of flowers, a bottle of wine, and a box of chocolates. Following her out to the driveway, I watch as she walks awkwardly, holding duffel bags in each arm.

"Yeah, Devin. Done." She rolls her eyes and continues putting her stuff in the car. The car, I might add, I bought her with the first profit that my shop turned.

"Do you even see what I'm holding, Nina?" I ask, thrusting my hands towards her.

"It's too late," she tells me, finally showing some emotion.

There are tears in her eyes and I wonder why. It's not like I'm the one leaving her. I still have no idea where any of this is coming from. "Too late? This is me telling you that I finally have the time. Babe, we're gonna live our lives."

"I've been living, Devin." She stomps her foot. "It's you who's had your head up your ass at that goddamn tattoo shop."

That's it. My stomach drops, and I see for the first time the ungrateful bitch she's become. I feel anger overtake me. "That goddamn tattoo shop has provided you with a good life, Nina," I yell.

Throwing the stuff down I have in my hands, I let it smash into a million pieces and watch it roll towards the car. Just like my life, it's a jumbled up mess of shattered hopes and a river full of broken dreams.

.

Made in the USA
Monee, IL
22 September 2022

14476288R00114